"I have been lo... ...g ... company for a long time, and I most certainly don't need you to bail me out."

Ethan placed the decanter on a side table and walked toward her. Kayla stood up ramrod straight. She refused to be bullied by Ethan and was determined to stand up to him even though butterflies were jumping around in her stomach at his nearness. She took a deep breath and calmed herself.

"No, I don't imagine you need me just yet." Ethan's fierce brown eyes focused on hers, and Kayla found she couldn't turn away from his piercing gaze that was drenched with hunger. "But you want me."

Kayla swallowed hard.

"Oh, yes." He watched Kayla nervously look downward. "You want me, but you're afraid to show it. That's all right. I have no problem going after what I want." Ethan grabbed Kayla by the shoulders, and his mouth slammed down on hers, stealing her breath and fracturing her thoughts into a million pieces. Before she knew what was happening, he had her up against the bookshelves and was pressing his body against her. He cupped the back of her head as his mouth kissed her with fervor.

Books by Yahrah St. John

Kimani Romance

Never Say Never
Risky Business of Love
Playing for Keeps
This Time for Real
If You So Desire
Two to Tango
Need You Now

YAHRAH ST. JOHN

is the author of nine books and numerous short stories. A graduate of Hyde Park Career Academy, she earned a Bachelor of Arts degree in English from Northwestern University.

Her books have garnered four-star ratings from *RT Book Reviews,* Rawsistaz Reviewers, Romance in Color and numerous book clubs. A member of Romance Writers of America, St. John is an avid reader of all genres. She enjoys the arts, cooking, traveling, basketball and adventure sports, but her true passion remains writing.

St. John lives in sunny Orlando, the City Beautiful.

Need You NOW

YAHRAH ST. JOHN

KIMANI
ROMANCE

Dedicated to my 2nd mother, Asilee Mitchell,
for imparting wisdom, comfort and care
when I needed a friend.

Recycling programs
for this product may
not exist in your area.

ISBN-13: 978-0-373-86238-2

NEED YOU NOW

Copyright © 2011 by Yahrah Yisrael

www.kimanipress.com

Printed in U.S.A.

Dear Reader,

I came up with the idea for *Need You Now* by watching *The Young and the Restless*. I loved the fact that the characters fought for their family business, a cosmetics company...and so an idea was born. Kayla, Shane and Courtney Adams would fight corporate raider Ethan Graham to save Adams Cosmetics. I'd stir the pot by having Ethan and Kayla form a marriage of convenience.

Stay tuned for more exciting drama in the second book of the Adams Family trilogy featuring Shane Adams and saucy *perfumier* Gabrielle Burton.

Spoiler alert: I introduced rival company Jax Cosmetics—owned by Andrew Jackson—in *Need You Now*. He will play a major role in the second and third books.

Feel free to visit my website, www.yahrahstjohn.com, for the latest updates. Contact me via email at Yahrah@yahrahstjohn.com, become a fan on Facebook or follow me on Twitter, twitter.com/yahrahstjohn.

Best wishes,

Yahrah St. John

This hasn't been an easy year physically, so I would be remiss if I didn't thank the people who've encouraged me to keep writing in the face of life's big obstacles.

Thank you to my Dad Austin Mitchell for being a rock of strength, Beatrice Astwood for her warmth and support and Demetrea Bishop, who is truly part of my family. And of course, I have to thank my girls Tonya Conway, Dimitra Astwood, Therolyn Rodgers and Tiffany Griffin—You keep me grounded! And my special friends: Bhushan Sukrham and Kiara Ashanti.

Lots of love to my readers for all their support.

Chapter 1

"Adams Cosmetics is in trouble," Michael Cartwright said during an emergency Monday-morning meeting with the executive members of the board. As CFO, he was privy to the finances and knew what dire straits the company was in.

Present were Kayla Adams, Shane Adams and Courtney Adams, along with several high-level executives.

"How bad is it?" Kayla asked, tossing her silky mane of curls over her shoulder.

"We've lost revenue in the past consecutive six quarters," Michael answered. "Blame it on the economy or consumers just spending less at Christmas, but we've seen a drop-off the past year."

"What about our reserves?" Kayla suggested.

"We've already been dipping into those for well over a year to keep the company afloat. Add the lost revenue and we're going to have to start laying off staff," Michael replied.

Kayla shook her head. "I refuse to do that. The employees

of Adams Cosmetics are like members of the family. There has to be another way."

"Investors," her brother, Shane, said.

Michael nodded in agreement. "We can contact your parents on their cruise. I'm sure given the situation the company is in, they would agree to part with shares."

"Absolutely not!" Kayla stood up resolutely, walked to the conference-room window and folded her arms across her chest. "This company has been privately owned for over twenty years." Not to mention how it would look to her parents to know that their eldest child had lost a company it had taken their entire lifetime to build. Kayla just couldn't let it happen.

"Kayla, we're running out of options," her baby sister, Courtney, spoke up in a low, firm voice. She may have been the youngest and considered the prettiest, but she also had a degree in marketing and finance from Duke University.

"What about the new fragrance line you're developing?" Kayla threw out to Shane. He was the head chemist at Adams Cosmetics and was not only brilliant but handsome, as well. "That's sure to be a winner."

"Kayla, do you have any idea what it would cost to launch a new line?" Michael replied.

"Of course I do," she whipped back. "I'm not a novice, Michael." She'd been CEO for the past five years since her father retired. She was one of the youngest CEOs in the business and proud of it. She'd gotten her master's in business administration from Harvard and had studied Adams Cosmetics from the ground up.

When she was little, her father, Byron Adams, would bring her into the office with him. She loved cosmetics and loved the idea that just a little bit of makeup could transform a woman from an ugly duckling into a swan. Even though she wore very little makeup herself, having been blessed with exceptional mahogany skin from her father, she'd made it her life's work to know every intricate detail of each line and how they came into existence.

Michael smiled despite her tone. Kayla had a razor-sharp tongue that would test the best of men. "I recognize that, Kayla," he returned calmly. "But it's going to cost millions for the kind of campaign we would need to launch Shane's line, which quite frankly the company doesn't have."

"Michael is right," Shane agreed.

"Whose side are you on?"

"This company's," Shane returned and turned his hazel eyes on his sister. The rest of the executive members might kowtow to his big sister, but he was not one of them. "Everyone, can you give Kayla and me a moment alone?"

"Try not to break anything," Courtney whispered to her older brother on her way out the double doors of the conference room. She was used to them fighting like cats and dogs, and she was in no mood to be peacemaker.

"Never fear." Shane stood up and buttoned his Italian suit. "Kayla doesn't scare me."

Once the doors had closed, Kayla wasted no time laying into Shane. "How dare you?" she whispered angrily, folding her arms across her chest. "You're supposed to back me up."

"Not when you're being unreasonable."

"I am not." Kayla pouted even though she knew there was some semblance of truth to Shane's words. "I am trying to save this company."

"That's why we're all here, Kay," Shane replied, pointing to the door the executives had just left through. "You're not the only one who loves this company. Like you, I've been working here for as long as I can remember. It's in my blood, too."

Kayla inhaled sharply. "I'm sorry, Shane. It's not you I'm upset with. It's this entire situation. You know as well as I do that the vultures are going to be circling us. Once word leaks, they're going to be swarming, ready to acquire us at a moment's notice."

"Since when do you give up without a fight?"

"Honestly, I don't know how to get us out of this mess," Kayla replied. "I mean, what's Daddy going think?" Kayla lowered her head and braced it in her hands. She felt like a failure.

"Kayla—" Shane grabbed her chin and forced her to look up at him "—this company was in trouble long before you took over."

"That's not true."

Shane shook his head. Kayla was such a daddy's girl. She hated to think that perhaps their father had made some less-than-desirable decisions near the end of his tenure as CEO and that now his children were left to clean up his mess. Kayla had put a bandage on the bleeding by curbing spending and implementing cost-cutting measures on production, but even she couldn't stop the inevitable. They were facing financial ruin if they didn't take immediate action.

"It is, even though you refuse to admit it," Shane said. "We need private investors willing to part with some serious capital."

"And put it into a sinking ship?" Kayla huffed. "Who would be foolish enough to do that?"

"We've received an interesting offer," Daniel Walker, vice president of Graham International told Ethan Graham in a closed-door meeting on Tuesday at their corporate office.

"What do you have?" Ethan answered, standing up and

buttoning up his charcoal Italian suit. He walked over to his wet bar to pour himself a glass of water and drank liberally.

"We've been approached by the CFO of Adams Cosmetics on whether Graham International would entertain purchasing shares in Adams Cosmetics."

"Oh, really?" Ethan's brow rose inquiringly. He'd known the Adams family since he was a child. Byron Adams had worked at Graham International with his father before starting his own company. The Graham and Adams families had been close once.

Byron Adams had been the father Ethan had never had, probably because Carter Graham hadn't known what to do with a young son at the age of sixty. He'd been shocked when his forty-two-year-old wife announced she was pregnant with their first and only child, considering they'd tried for a number of years. She'd given birth to a healthy baby boy, but a late-in-life child was not what Carter had been looking for and it was evident in his treatment of Ethan.

Once when he'd won a lacrosse championship, he'd come home with his trophy eager to show his father how hard he'd worked, but Carter had been cold and indifferent. No matter how hard he tried to please him, Carter refused to give him any praise. But that had only made Ethan work harder to win his approval. His mother, Eleanor, had tried to show him enough love and affection for the both of them, but Ethan had never felt like Carter cared about him one way or the other.

Ethan supposed that's why he respected Byron Adams. Byron was a wonderful, attentive father who cared about his children. Ethan was admittedly jealous when he would spend the night over at the Adams's residence and see how much love they had for each other. He envied them.

Then everything changed. Byron left Graham International to start Adams Cosmetics, which had devastated his father. Carter considered it an act of betrayal on Byron's part and thus the divide between their families began. He'd thought after his father died, his relationship with Byron would return to normal, but Byron seemed to think Ethan was a carbon copy of his father. When Ethan would see Byron upon occasion, he was always civil, but the bond between them had been broken. Ethan had also lost his mother a few years after Carter's death, and he was now alone.

"Adams Cosmetics could go under," Daniel stated. He didn't believe in beating around the bush. Ethan knew him to be a straight shooter and he didn't intend on changing that one bit.

"Why? What happened?"

"They're in need of capital," Daniel replied, leaning forward in his chair. "If someone doesn't bail them out soon, they'll be out of business before the year is out. They've extended themselves as much as they can with the banks, and if they want to go forward with any of the new products Shane Adams is creating, they're going to need investors."

Ethan nodded. "Is Kayla Adams agreeable to an outsider investing in her company?" he inquired. Byron's eldest daughter was CEO of Adams Cosmetics and he doubted she would appreciate an outsider owning a piece of her pie. Matter of fact, she would be livid. Kayla had never liked Ethan since he'd declined her attempt at seventeen to lure him into bed. He'd been six years her senior, and having any kind of relationship at the time would have been completely inappropriate. Though now would be an entirely different matter altogether.

"I've heard she's amicable," Daniel returned. "If they don't get funds soon, they'll have to take the company public and submit an IPO. You and I both know that is not only costly, but the Adams family would also lose control of their company."

Ethan smiled. "I highly doubt she's accepting this lying down." Kayla Adams was a fighter.

"So are you open to buying the shares the Adams family might put on the market?"

"Of course, but I want more than a few shares. I want to own the majority interest," Ethan replied. If he was going to invest in a sinking ship, he needed complete control to bring it back from the brink of disaster. "Start inquiring with our bank on raising capital."

"Ethan, the Adams family will never give up control."

"Then find a loophole."

"You sure don't want much," Daniel returned, closing his file. "I wouldn't think you'd be so ruthless, considering your history with the family."

"You know me, Daniel. Since when have I ever let personal feelings get in the way of business? I want the whole pie or nothing at all, and this circumstance is no different."

"Understood."

"Treat this as extremely confidential," Ethan added. "I don't want word of this leaking out." He had to strike while the iron was hot and prevent any other corporate mammoths from snapping up Adams Cosmetics. Their cosmetics company would fit in nicely with Graham International, which specialized primarily in fashion and perfume but had a small cosmetics division.

"Absolutely." Daniel nodded and headed toward the door, but stopped short. "You know, Kayla Adams is going to consider your interest in the company as hostile. Especially considering you're asking for majority shares."

"Oh, I know," Ethan responded. Kayla was not going to cooperate with him. In fact, since that incident in the stables when she was seventeen, Kayla had made a point of keeping a wide berth from Ethan every time they met. At first he'd thought he was imagining it. He assumed Kayla was embarrassed at her juvenile seduction attempt, but after the last party they attended a few years back, when she'd pointedly refused to dance with him, Ethan knew he wasn't. How could she go from wanting him to not wanting to be near him? Ethan suspected that Kayla was as far from immune to him as she portrayed. "I will handle Kayla."

"Are you sure about that?" Daniel asked.

Ethan chuckled. Kayla was a spitfire, and she wouldn't take kindly to Graham International owning a stake in Adams Cosmetics, but Ethan was determined.

"Daddy, what are you doing back?" Kayla asked when she came down to breakfast the next morning and found her father sitting at the dining room table. It was a beautiful spring day in mid-March, and the flowers on the family's eleven-bedroom estate in Atlanta's Buckhead division were blooming. But Kayla didn't feel as cheery as the weather. "And where's Mom?"

"Went to the spa," her father replied, looking up from his paper. "She wasn't too pleased that we cut our extended vacation short."

"Of course she would be upset. You promised."

"I know, but once I heard about Adams Cosmetics, I had to come back."

"So you came back because of the company?" Kayla asked thoughtfully and rose from the table to serve herself some yogurt and fresh fruit from the buffet table behind them. Victor, their butler, always had a delicious spread for breakfast.

"Don't be upset, Kay," her father said, using the nickname

he'd given her as a child. It was usually when he wanted her to do things his way, but it wouldn't be that way this time.

"You don't think I can save the company on my own?" Kayla asked as she sat down with her plate. She reached for the coffee carafe in the center of the table and poured herself a cup. She brought it to her lips and took a sip. It was as she liked it, strong and black, much like her men.

"No, of course not." Byron rose from his chair and came to sit beside her. "That's not it at all. I just know how much you want Adams Cosmetics to stay in the family."

"It's how it's always been," Kayla responded. "And now, Shane and Courtney want to bring in 'investors.'" She used her hands to make quotation marks. "They want to bring outsiders into the company."

"It's what has to be done."

"Then why did you never do it?" Kayla returned, a little too harshly for her liking.

"Because I was a fool," Byron admitted to his daughter. "I didn't want to admit that I could be wrong. I don't want to see the same thing happen to you."

"You weren't wrong, Daddy. This is a family business," Kayla persisted.

"One that could go bankrupt due to the bad decisions I made in the past. Kay, if you want to save Adams Cosmetics, we're going to have to do what needs to be done and sell some of our shares."

"I can't let you do this. You and Mama started this company. How does Mama feel about this?" Kayla inquired. She doubted her mother would be happy to hear that they could be losing a part of the business it had taken them a lifetime to build. Not to mention the long working days and late nights they'd endured during the early days to make the company a success.

"She has given me carte blanche to do whatever is necessary."

Kayla shook her head in resignation. "I just can't believe it's come down to this, selling off our shares for the almighty dollar."

"It will keep the company solvent. More than that, it will give you the much-needed capital to invest in the new fragrance line Shane has created, as well as expand our skincare line. These are all projects you've wanted to do for a very long time, but didn't have the finances."

Kayla respected her father's opinion and knew he was right, but it hurt all the same. "Okay." She shrugged her shoulders. "You've convinced me. Now what?"

"Now what?" her father asked, stroking her cheek. "Once the company is back on its feet, it can finally allow you to have a personal life and give your mother and me our first grandchild."

"Children!" Kayla huffed and pushed back her chair. "Where did that come from?" She took another sip of her coffee.

"It's about time you started working on a family, old girl." Her father patted her shoulder. "You're not getting any younger."

Kayla's mouth upturned. "Thanks a lot, Dad." She knew she was getting up there in years. At thirty-four years old, she was no spring chicken in the female reproductive world. Until now, she'd never really thought about having a child. She'd always been so focused on her career. Sure, there had been a number of men with whom she'd had casual affairs, but none of them had held a candle to her first crush, Ethan Graham.

She knew it was silly that she compared the men she'd dated to Ethan, but compare she had. Ever since he'd returned from boarding school at the ripe age of fifteen and picked her up when she'd fallen off her pony at nine years old and kissed her knee, she'd been infatuated. And as she got older, it only grew stronger. How could she forget those six-pack abs in swim shorts and those muscular arms as they swum in her family's pool? Ayden Turner, her ex-boyfriend, had tried but failed to live up to Ethan's dark good looks and rippled physique.

She'd seen Ethan in the years since and had effectively kept him at a distance. She'd had to. She'd made a fool of herself when she'd come on to him when she was seventeen and he'd turned her down flat. And since then, he'd dated a string of beauties and wealthy socialites, so even if she would have approached him again, he was too full of himself to even notice. So she focused on her career.

"I didn't mean that how it sounded." Her father spoke at her silence. "You know you have always been the light of my life, Kayla, and I only want what's best for you."

"I know that, Daddy. And maybe one day your wish will come true."

"I've put together a great list of potential investors," Michael said when he called another meeting of the executive committee of Adams Cosmetics on Thursday morning, "and quietly started putting the word out that we're looking for capital."

Kayla perused the names on the list and was startled to see Ethan Graham's name. "Ethan Graham," she said aloud, shocked. That's the last name she'd expected to see. Hadn't she just been thinking about him this morning?

"Of course," Shane said. "I gave Michael his name. Ethan is a former family friend and he might be willing to lend a hand."

"You know Daddy's not going to like this idea," Kayla responded. Actually, she knew how *she* felt. She hated the idea. She didn't want arrogant Ethan Graham to have any part of the family business.

Shane's brow furrowed. "Well, Dad isn't running this company, you are. Whatever beef he had with Ethan's father should never have translated outside of business. Ethan used to be practically one of the family."

"Well, he's not now." The moment the words were out of her mouth, Kayla realized how juvenile she must have sounded. Shane and Courtney were both looking at her strangely.

"What do you have against Ethan?" Shane asked. "He's a brilliant businessman."

"Oh, leave her alone," Courtney said, seeing how flushed Kayla's mahogany skin was becoming. She may have been a few years younger, but even she had seen the monumental crush Kayla had had on Ethan back in the day. Trust her brother, being a man, not to notice.

"Have you thought about how many shares you're all going to put on the market?" Michael inquired, breaking into the sibling conversation.

"What do you mean you all?" Kayla inquired. "I imagined the shares would be minimal." She wanted to keep as many as possible.

"The shares have to be significant in order to get an investor interested. I spoke with your father this morning and he and your mother, Shane and Courtney will sell 12.5 shares each and you would retain 25 percent as president."

Why hadn't her father told her about this decision at breakfast? "What about you two?" Kayla looked at Shane. "This hardly seems fair."

"We know how much Adams Cosmetics means to you," Shane responded. "And we're fine with the arrangement."

Kayla pondered Shane's words. "Okay, I can accept that, but that would potentially give a single investor 37.5 percent interest of Adams Cosmetics."

"True, but think of the reward," Michael responded. "Or the shares could be divided among several investors."

"Money isn't everything," Kayla returned.

"Since when?" Courtney asked. She'd seen the financials. Now was not the time to play it safe.

"Fine." Kayla's mouth went into a grim line. She hated this, but she didn't have much choice; she was in the minority.

"How are you coming with raising funds?" Ethan asked Daniel later that afternoon.

"Slowly," Daniel replied. "Because Adams Cosmetics is a private company, their financial statements aren't public record, so the bank is hesitant to lend funds."

"Continue to work on it. If necessary, I'll place a call to the head of finance. If they want to keep Graham International as a customer, they will back this venture."

"Sure thing," Daniel said on his way out.

It left Ethan time alone to peruse a dossier on the Adams family. Over the past several years Graham International had expanded into several overseas markets, which had taken Ethan out of the country. He needed to catch up on what the Adamses were up to.

The youngest, Courtney Adams, was spokeswoman for the Adams Cosmetics line. But she was also a force to be reckoned with. She had a degree in marketing and finance. Yet there was an impetuous streak in her. When she'd run off with her boyfriend to Vegas for a quickie marriage when she was eighteen, Byron had reined in his hotheaded daughter and had the marriage annulled.

Shane Adams might be the middle child, but he was by no means overshadowed by the eldest or youngest. Shane was a brilliant chemist—he had been classically trained in Paris and was now vice president. He'd revolutionized Adams Cosmetics with the development of the skincare line when he was only twenty-five. Ethan was sure that with proper funding, the new fragrance line he was developing would be a success.

And finally there was Kayla Adams, CEO. Gone was the awkward young girl with long gangly legs. The Kayla he saw in the photo was breathtakingly beautiful. Kayla had matured into a cool, sophisticated businesswoman.

He turned the page and focused on her accomplishments. Poised and driven to succeed at all costs, Kayla had started working at Adams Cosmetics when she was fifteen and never left. She became CEO of Adams Cosmetics at twenty-nine when Byron stepped down. Her decision-making skills were said to be exemplary, which would be both an asset and a curse.

Kayla wasn't going to give up control of Adams Cosmetics easily. That's why Ethan had to be ruthless and insist they sign over additional shares. Right now they were only offering 37.5 percent to investors, but that was not going to do. Graham International must have controlling interest in Adams Cosmetics. It was the only way.

Chapter 2

"Are we attending the Tyler Perry movie premiere this evening?" Courtney asked her big sister Saturday morning as they prepared to square off in a game of tennis on the family estate. The Adams family estate was equipped with a pool, basketball and tennis court as well as a stable for the horses that Kayla used to ride during championships.

The sisters had dressed for battle, Kayla in a pink-and-gray tennis dress that hit her thigh while Courtney wore a purple tank top and tennis skirt. Both wore their hair in unsophisticated ponytails.

"Of course," Kayla returned, stretching her arms behind her. "We have to present a united front to the world. Just because word is out that Adams Cosmetics is in trouble doesn't mean we are going to slink off into a corner somewhere."

"I never thought we were," Courtney responded. "We're fighters. So when is the limo picking us up?" As spokeswoman for Adams Cosmetics, Courtney attended every public function.

"Six p.m." Kayla picked up her racket from the ground and headed to her side of the court.

"Oh, I'll be ready."

"Are you ready to lose, little sis?" Kayla yelled over the court. "Because I'm about to give you a spanking."

"Those are big words for someone who's five years older than me." Courtney laughed as she removed her jacket and tossed it on the green.

"Oh, I'm going to make you eat those words." Kayla chuckled. She gave an overhead serve and sent the tennis ball flying in the air.

They played a hearty game before coming to a deuce.

"You realize once I serve, I have the advantage?" Courtney yelled over the net.

"Enough talk, Courtney. Let's get on with it," Kayla responded. Courtney served the ball and Kayla hit it with such force that Courtney had to go flying to reach it. But she still missed the point. "Whatcha gotta say about that?" Kayla teased as she did a victory dance.

"Oh, shut up," Courtney said. "Can we just agree to disagree?" she asked, walking toward the net.

"Sure." Kayla smiled back at her sister. "If you'll agree I'm the better player."

"Like hell I will."

"Then we'll have to have a rematch." Kayla ruffled Courtney's hair with her hands. "Now come on, I'm starved and it looks like Victor put out a great spread." As a longtime employee, Victor was like a member of the Adams family and always took care of them. He'd put out a platter of sandwiches, pasta salad, fruit and a pitcher of ice-cold lemonade in the gazebo next to the tennis court.

"And I'm ready for it," Courtney said as they strolled toward the gazebo.

Once there, they piled up their crystal plates with sandwiches, salad and fruit and sat down to the table.

"You're very quiet," Courtney remarked.

"I'm not happy about having to bring outside investors into Adams Cosmetics," Kayla said, and then put up her hand. "And before you start enumerating the reasons why this is the right thing to do, don't. I know what's at stake, but I'm still disappointed that I couldn't prevent this from happening."

"You've done everything in your power, Kayla, to preserve Daddy's vision, but even you aren't Superwoman."

Kayla gave a halfhearted smile. "Since when? When you were little you believed I could do anything." She could easily remember Courtney following her around like a puppy dog and being annoyed that her little sister wanted to hang around her teenage friends.

Courtney laid her hands over her hips. "And I still do. There isn't anything you can't do when you put your mind to it, Kayla, and that's why I know you're going to make this work."

"Thanks, doll." Kayla patted her hand and then proceeded to take a big bite of the chicken salad on croissant that Victor had made for them.

"No matter who the investor is?" Courtney asked, and placed a forkful of pasta salad in her mouth.

Kayla wiped her mouth with the nearby napkin. "What do you mean by that?"

"Ethan Graham?" The name landed like a missile in the air.

"What about him?" Kayla looked down.

"Oh, nothing." Courtney shrugged. "It just seemed like back in the day, you may have had a thing for the man."

Kayla laughed nervously. "That's utterly ridiculous."

"Is it?" Courtney asked, twisting open the cap on her water bottle and taking a generous sip. "The man is handsome as sin. Are you blind?"

Kayla inhaled sharply just thinking about him. Was it obvious even to her sister that she'd once had feelings for Ethan that had gone unrequited?

"No, I'm not blind…" Kayla responded. She remembered every detail about the man, even if it had been a year or so since she'd seen him. Who could forget those smoldering dark eyes of his or that broad expanse of shoulders? She sure couldn't. She had fantasies about what it would be like to have his arms wrapped around her.

"But I feel there is a 'but' coming in there," Courtney finished her sentence.

"I don't feel that Graham International is the right fit for us," Kayla replied. "They have their hands in so many markets—clothing, perfume, leather goods. Their cosmetics division is small."

"Which is why Ethan will jump at the chance of being part of Adams Cosmetics. Why are you so against this, Kayla?"

"I'm not, but there are tons of investors out there. Why does it have to be Ethan?"

"Because he'll have not only a monetary investment but a personal stake, as well. I doubt Ethan wants the company to fail."

"Are you sure about that?" Kayla asked. "Look at the way Dad treats him. He's always thought that the apple didn't fall too far from the tree."

"That's because of what happened with Dad and Ethan's father. It doesn't mean Ethan is as ruthless as his old man."

"Courtney, you are so naive. Ethan Graham is exactly his father's son, how else do you think he grew Graham International? He has to be as cutthroat as Carter Graham ever was, if not worse."

"Everything is coming along nicely," Daniel told Ethan later that morning after a late lunch and game of racquetball. They were sitting in Ethan's study and discussing his strategy.

"So you've put the word out to potential investors that Adams Cosmetics is mine?" Ethan asked.

"Yes," Daniel stated. "I got my hands on their short list. I will make some confidential calls and advise you are prepared to match any offer an investor may make for shares in AC."

"Good." Ethan nodded. "And the bank?"

"Still on the fence."

"Then it's time I place a call to Perry Lee," Ethan said, rising from the sofa and walking toward his desk.

"You're going to call Perry on a Saturday?" Daniel asked.

"Why not?" Ethan asked. "My banker should always be ready for the unexpected." Once he'd called Perry and asked him to wire a quarter of a million dollars to Monte Carlo for a poker game he was playing. Perry had thought he was out of his mind, but when Ethan had doubled the money and wired back the cash, Perry had learned to never underestimate him.

Daniel shrugged.

Ethan dialed Perry's personal cell phone number. "Perry, it's Ethan."

Daniel listened to snippets of the conversation and knew that Ethan would soon go for the jugular.

"We need to discuss this Adams Cosmetics deal…hmm… yes, I understand I am asking for a large sum…The bank is concerned about the risks…Have you ever known Graham International to default on a loan…Then there should be no problem with you getting this deal approved…Well, if you don't think you can handle it…Then perhaps I should start looking at other banks…Great, I look forward to hearing from you. Please do tell Annette I said hello and enjoy the rest of your weekend."

Daniel watched Ethan walk back to the couch with a smug expression. "Now that's how you get things done."

"A threat here, a threat there…"

"Perry just needed an incentive to get the job done."

"If you don't mind my asking, why is this so important to you?"

"If not for my father, there would never have been an Adams Cosmetics. Carter refused to compromise and so our fathers went their separate ways. We should have all been one great big happy family. The times I spent with the Adams family were some of the best of my life. There was room for everyone at the top, but my father was too pig-headed to see that."

"And now you're trying to make things right?" Daniel inquired. "It sounds altruistic, but I think there's more to it than that, otherwise you wouldn't be asking for majority interest."

Ethan rubbed his jaw. "Well, yes, I will get something out of this arrangement."

"When are you going to make your move?"

"Soon. In the meantime I need to get ready for the Tyler

Perry premiere this evening." He was sure a certain statuesque beauty would be present for the festivities.

Kayla stared back at her reflection in the pedestal mirror
in her room. She was Daddy's girl and looked just like him,
while Shane and Courtney were the spitting image of their
fair-skinned mother. She looked darn good in a one-shoulder
black charmeuse gown that ruched tightly at her waist and
had a front slit from floor to thigh. The silky fabric clung
to her every curve. No one was going to miss seeing her
this evening. Was it a little over the top for her? Yes. Courtney was usually the provocateur, while Kayla dressed more
conservatively. So why was she pulling out all the stops tonight? Kayla told herself she was dressing this way for her
own benefit, but in the back of her mind, she knew she was
dressing this way because a certain someone was sure to
attend tonight's event and she wanted to show him what he
could have had.

"You ready, sis?" Shane knocked at her door.

"Come in."

"Wow!" Shane's jaw dropped.

Kayla smiled at the bemused expression on Shane's face.
"You like?" She twirled around.

"You look gorgeous, but I might have to beat the men
away with a stick." Shane came to stand behind her and
Kayla glanced at the reflection of them in the mirror.

Her brother was a tall drink of water in any woman's
book. He stood several inches taller than her five-foot-nine
inches and had the most stunning pair of hazel eyes she'd
ever laid eyes on. They never knew where he'd inherited
them from, as both their parents had brown eyes. But Kayla
was sure that pair had seduced many a women. And looking

as dapper as he did in his tuxedo, she was sure Shane would be on the prowl tonight.

"Let's go." Kayla tucked her arm in his and headed for the door. When they walked down the winding staircase to the bottom of the foyer, their parents, Byron and Elizabeth, and Courtney were waiting for them.

Kayla knew some people would think it was crazy that she and her siblings hadn't moved out of their parents' home, but why should they move? They were a close-knit family that did everything together, and until one of them got hitched there was no need to move out. There were more than enough rooms in the eleven-room mansion that each of them had their own wing and plenty of privacy to come and go as they pleased.

"Mom." Kayla kissed her mother. "You look beautiful." Her salt-and-pepper hair was swept up in an elegant chignon and she wore a metallic ruffle belted jacket over a simple sheath with pearls.

"And you, missy—" Kayla glanced at her sister "—will be the belle of the ball as always." The black animal-print gown clung to Courtney's size-four figure before sweeping out like a mermaid's tail to the floor. Trust her sister to show up her attempt to be a little mischievous with her front slit.

"Well, you're not too bad yourself." Courtney laughed. "I wholeheartedly approve."

"Enough with all the compliments," their father said from the front door. "We have to get going. We're already late."

"Hey, you can't hurry perfection," Kayla responded. "It takes time, Daddy, to look this good."

"Amen!" Courtney chorused on their way out of the door.

When they arrived at the hotel where the premiere was being held, it was already in full swing. Actors, directors and the cream of Atlanta society were already milling around the ballroom in grand attire.

"Tonight would be the perfect night to mention your new perfume line," Kayla whispered to Shane as they exited the vehicle. "You know, generate some buzz."

"I agree," Shane responded in her ear.

"So what's new for Adams Cosmetics?" a reporter for the local newspaper asked once they hit the red carpet.

"It's funny you should ask," Kayla said, laughing, "because Adams Cosmetics will be debuting a fragrance in the coming months."

"Perfume, that's a new arena for Adams Cosmetics," the reporter replied.

"True, but Adams Cosmetics has always been about beauty," Kayla stated. "We're in the business of making women feel good about themselves. We already have shampoos, conditioners and body products."

"Perfume is a natural progression for us to expand into," Shane added.

"I'm sure the public is eager to see what you have in store for us."

"And we look forward to bringing them quality products," Kayla replied.

Once they were done with the press bit, the Adams family separated and worked the room. Her parents went in the direction of some old friends while Courtney continued her due diligence with the press.

Kayla watched her younger sister toss her hair around for a photo op. "That went well," Kayla said to Shane at her side.

"Yes, it did," Shane said. "Now all I have to do is deliver a knockout fragrance."

"Which you will." Kayla squeezed his shoulder. "You

know I have absolute faith in you. So let's talk to Perry Lee. He's the head of one of the banks I'd like to approach."

"Kay, can you for once not think about business and let your hair down and have some fun? I sure intend to." Shane went rushing off toward a group of beautiful women nearby that were ogling his good looks.

The dress was her letting her hair down, Kayla thought to herself. Kayla glanced around the room anxiously, wringing her hands. Why was she so nervous? It wasn't like she hadn't been to a hundred of these events before. Deep down, she knew why. Ethan Graham was expected to attend. All the gossip blogs were talking about who the elusive bachelor would attend the gala with. Would he be like his father and wait until later in life to marry? Kayla didn't know.

She recalled their encounter in France a few years ago, when she'd made polite pleasantries and retreated as fast as she could from his overpowering male presence. But recently, despite all her best efforts, the man seemed to be haunting her daytime thoughts and nighttime dreams. It had to be because he'd suddenly shown interest in Adams Cosmetics, because she refused to believe it could be something more.

Kayla was happy when her eyes fixed on a certain redheaded entertainment reporter working the room with her cameraman. "Piper!" She waved enthusiastically at her oldest and dearest friend. Piper was petite, barely reaching five feet, with shockingly vibrant red hair and freckles spread over her fair skin, but no one could deny that when she was on-screen, you couldn't take your eyes off her.

"Kay." Piper stopped short when she crossed the room to her friend. "I'm loving the dress!" She turned to her cameraman. "Let's take a quick break. I'll find you in a bit." He nodded before walking away.

Kayla blushed, but gave a twirl. "You like?'

"Oh, yeah." Piper nodded. "Do you have your eye on someone tonight?" she asked, glancing around the room.

"Why would you say that?" Kayla chuckled nervously.

"Because you never show all the goods." Piper motioned to the side slit.

"What's wrong with being a little sexy?" Kayla inquired. "There's a time and a place for it."

"And clearly tonight is the night." Piper laughed. "Let's grab some champagne. They have the good stuff." She tugged at Kayla's arm.

"Sure, sure." Kayla glanced over her shoulder uneasily. It felt as if someone was watching her, but when she turned around and found no one she brushed it off and joined Piper at the bar.

"She's here," Ethan stated from across the dance floor. Photos had done Kayla little justice. They didn't capture just how sexy and beautiful the executive truly was. Luscious full lips, a mass of sexy wavy hair and legs that went on for miles. Ethan could feel his body temperature rising just looking at her.

He watched Kayla glide to the bar in a delicious confection of a dress. When she walked, it showed a very nice expanse of leg that was causing blood to rush through his veins. He watched as she sipped her champagne flute. Oh, how he wished he was that glass to receive those full lips of hers.

"She is, as are all the Adamses," Daniel returned.

"Of course." Ethan nodded, drinking his scotch. "And I think it's time I reacquainted myself with Ms. Adams."

"Good luck," Daniel said as Ethan strolled toward the women.

* * *

Kayla and Piper were discussing Piper's latest report about an up-and-coming actress who couldn't seem to get off drugs and alcohol. Suddenly, Kayla felt the hairs on the back of her neck stand at attention.

Kayla swung around and found herself staring up into a pair of dark brown eyes that were intensely focused on her. Although she'd known Ethan Graham might attend, she'd wanted their first meeting to be on her terms, so she could be prepared. Not like this—she wasn't prepared to have the full magnitude of those sexy brown eyes on her. And the years, well, they had been good to him. She surmised he'd just hit forty, but that didn't matter, because he was still the most magnificent specimen of a man she'd ever laid her eyes on.

Ethan still had a sinfully sculpted face with a square jaw that would make any woman weak at the knees. He towered over her at six foot three and looked debonair in a black tuxedo minus a tie. What was the saying, the suit made the man? In this case, it was the opposite—the man absolutely made the suit look good.

Piper was the first to speak. She was used to being around gorgeous celebrities as an entertainment reporter. "Ethan Graham." She extended her hand. "Pleasure to see you again."

"You, as well, Piper." Ethan smiled at the redhead. "It's been a while. I remember you running around in your knickers with Kayla."

Immediately Kayla flushed at the memory of Ethan catching her and Piper running around in their boy-short pajamas when he and his father stopped by for a visit to their house.

"So very gentlemanly of you to remind us, Ethan." Kayla finally found her voice.

Ethan smiled broadly, showing a perfect smile and straight white teeth. He'd ruffled her feathers. "Well, I'm no gentleman." His voice was low and masculine.

"I've heard that." Piper jumped into the action. "The paparazzi do seem fascinated with your dating exploits."

"And it's because of my exploits that celebrity reporters such as yourself do so well, yes?" Ethan responded, taking a sip of his scotch.

"Touché." Piper nodded.

"Can I get you ladies another drink?" Ethan asked cordially as he noticed their flutes were empty.

"I'm fine," Piper answered, "but Kayla here could use one." She could feel tension emanating out of Kayla's every pore. "Matter of fact, why don't I leave you to catch up? I have to mingle and find my cameraman."

Kayla glared at Piper. She couldn't believe she was deserting her and leaving her alone with him, but she was. Piper was already making her way through the crowd while Ethan was fetching the bartender.

When he'd finished ordering, he returned to face Kayla. "Well, that just leaves the two of us." He smiled down at her.

"Unfortunately." She tried to calm the shivers that were running through her at his breathtaking grin.

"Now who is being impolite?" Ethan's brow rose.

"C'mon Ethan, you and I haven't seen each other in years and have nothing to catch up on."

"What if I'd like to change that?" Ethan handed her a glass of champagne from the bartender.

Kayla chuckled but accepted the flute. "Oh, really?"

"Yes. I think you could use a man like me right now."

"A man like you?" Kayla swallowed the lump in her throat. Could Ethan tell she was still attracted to him?

Ethan watched the color drain from Kayla's face. She

thought he meant sexually and he did. But clearly she wasn't ready for a little flirtation, so he switched gears. "Adams Cosmetics is in need of capital, correct? And since I am the head of Graham International, it might behoove us to talk. You can tell me what's going on with Adams Cosmetics. I think I caught wind of some new fragrance line Shane is developing?"

Kayla blinked a moment to snap herself out of the daze she was in. Of course he meant business. Ethan Graham hadn't been interested in her when she was seventeen and tonight was no different. He was used to gorgeous celebrities like his ex-girlfriend Noelle Warner. Noelle was a beautiful, Oscar-winning actress with a killer figure who was rumored to change partners just as easily as she changed roles.

"And why would I do that?" Kayla asked. "I don't want Graham International to have any part of Adams Cosmetics."

Ethan didn't like her tone. "And what's wrong with my company?"

"It's what's wrong with every large international company. It's a cold, unfeeling, impersonal corporate mammoth. Adams Cosmetics is a family business that puts out quality product."

"So does Graham International," Ethan huffed. "We wouldn't have gotten to where we are without it. How do you think I've expanded into clothing, perfume and leather goods in the overseas markets without producing quality product?"

"Precisely," Kayla said. "You're doing so much that you've lost focus. I care about my employees and consider them part of the family. I bet you don't even know half the people that work for you."

"And you do?"

"I know every person who works for me," Kayla stated emphatically. She was proud that she was an approachable boss. Although Adams Cosmetics was a boutique company with several hundred employees, Kayla had always made a point to get to know everyone who reported directly to her, as well as the secretaries, cafeteria workers and janitors who kept the company running smoothly.

"Well, perhaps that's the problem," Ethan responded. "Perhaps you need to focus more on business and less on being liked by your employees." As soon as he said the words, Ethan wished he could take them back. They were harsh.

"How dare you? You know nothing about me, less than nothing!" Kayla was livid, and forced herself to put the champagne glass down on the bar rather than throw it in his face. She stormed toward the nearest exit, which just happened to be the terrace.

It was a chilly spring night and couldn't have been more than fifty degrees, but Kayla didn't care. She needed the cold air as her blood was boiling. Kayla started when she heard footsteps. Ethan was behind her. His large looming presence filled the ballroom doorway and gave her system one hell of a jolt. She hadn't expected him to follow her.

"Go away!" She turned her back. "I want to be alone."

Ethan didn't listen and came toward her. "Listen, I'm sorry, Kayla," he said. "I crossed the line a moment ago."

"You sure did." Kayla didn't look back at him. She hated that she'd lost her cool. She wanted to show Ethan that she was no longer affected by him, but instead she was acting like a schoolgirl. She was a businesswoman after all, and used to healthy rival talk, just not from him.

"I did, but you must realize that your company needs me now," he whispered softly in her ear.

When had he come so close? Kayla instantly moved a step away. "My company doesn't need you. I will find other investors. I don't need you or your interference."

Ethan refused to have a conversation with Kayla with her back to him. He laid his hand on her shoulder and gently spun her around to look him. "Are you sure about that?"

Kayla's skin was tingling from where Ethan was holding her; she didn't want to look at him. Heat was emanating from his body and stirring sensations deep inside her. She could feel her breasts begin to swell and a warm sensation begin to spread through the lower half of her body. It was the same heat she'd felt inside, which was why she'd had to escape, but a powerful force propelled her to look up at him. And when she did, she wished she hadn't. His dark brown eyes smoldered with...dare she say passion? And it scared her, so she closed her eyes. *Had she gotten it wrong? Was Ethan Graham interested in her?*

"Look at me Kayla." Ethan's index finger hooked under her jaw, forcing her to raise her head and meet his gaze again.

When she opened her eyes, Ethan was looking at her so intently that it was wreaking havoc on her body.

"I think it's time I finally found out how you taste." Ethan was ready to fully savor what those sweet full lips of hers had in store. He lowered his head, intent on having his heart's desire, when another couple came out onto the deck.

"Sorry, sorry," the man said when he realized he'd interrupted something. But it was already too late. The moment was broken and Kayla quickly pulled away from Ethan and ran inside.

As she stumbled into the ballroom, Kayla realized she'd almost succumbed to Ethan's world-famous charm. How had he shattered her defenses so quickly? She'd thought she was immune to him. Clearly, she'd been wrong.

Outside, Ethan's mouth widened into a grin. Kayla Adams still wanted him? He was glad, because tonight she'd lit a flame inside him that no woman had done. He hadn't been with a woman in well over six months. That may not seem long for some men, but for him it was. He had a high sex drive that hadn't been met by any of the women he'd encountered, so he'd stopped trying. Until Kayla. Was it the soft luscious curls that hung down her sleek back or that she had just the right amount of curves: high pert breasts and a round shapely bottom? Whatever it may be, she'd aroused him and now he had to have it all. The woman and her business.

Chapter 3

Kayla knew what she had to do. On Monday, she scheduled a lunch meeting with Michael to discuss prospects.

"How's the progress coming with finding investors?"

"Interest is definitely there," Michael replied, closing the folder he was reading, "But as I indicated, the amount of shares you're willing to sell is vital to any deal."

"I need you to start setting up some meetings," Kayla replied.

"What's the rush?"

The rush was she didn't want Graham International anywhere near Adams Cosmetics, or Ethan Graham anywhere near her. The easiest way to prevent a catastrophe from happening and having to grovel to him to save her company was to find another investor.

"The sooner we get moving on this, the better. I don't want word spreading like wildfire."

They were perusing their menus when Andrew Jackson

and his stepdaughter, Monica Jackson, approached their table. Had they been lurking in the shadows listening to their conversation and smelled blood?

"Kayla Adams," Andrew Jackson greeted her. "How are you, darling?"

Kayla hated Andrew's fake country accent. It went right along with his smarmy slicked-back hair and cowboy boots. He towered over the table at six foot six, but he did not intimidate Kayla. Andrew Jackson owned Jax Cosmetics, which was one of their competitors. Up until the economy went bad, Adams Cosmetics had consistently beat Jax Cosmetics in sales in the Southeast.

Although a smaller operation than Adams Cosmetics, Jax Cosmetics was showing rapid signs of growth. If Andrew and his stepdaughter Monica, who ran the company, knew they were in trouble, who knew what shenanigans they would pull?

"I'm well, thank you, Andrew. Monica," Kayla inclined her head to his stepdaughter standing beside him. Although she might seem mousy at five foot three in a black trouser suit with designer glasses and a simple ponytail, Monica was a she-devil. Kayla supposed she had to be aggressive given that Andrew had always wanted his son, Jasper, to run the company, so Monica constantly had to prove herself. Jasper wanted nothing to do with his father and his stepfamily and had gone to live with his mother when he was a young boy. No one had heard from or seen him since.

Kayla was thankful that her relationship with her father was totally different. "Can I do something for you, Andrew?" Kayla inquired.

"No." Andrew shook his head. "I wanted to congratulate you. We weren't able to make it to Tyler Perry's premiere as we were in the South of France, but we heard that Adams

Cosmetics might be starting a new fragrance line. That's quite ambitious, given the state of the economy."

"True, but with great risk comes the biggest reward," Kayla responded.

"Good luck," Monica replied. "You'll need it." She stalked away, and Andrew chuckled as he followed her to their table.

Kayla turned back around to face Michael. "See what we're dealing with? They are waiting for us to fail. We have to strike now. I need you to set up those meetings immediately."

"Will do."

"Are you in a better mood than you were on Saturday?" Daniel asked when he ran into Ethan in the hallway of Graham International on Monday morning.

Ethan laughed. He had been rather perturbed about being interrupted when he was about to kiss Kayla. He'd been on the cusp of seeing exactly what it was he'd passed up all those years ago in the stables. Of course, now things were different. Kayla Adams was a grown woman, a woman that he desperately wanted in his bed.

"Yes, I am. Today is a new day." As he'd drifted off to sleep, Ethan had determined to pull out all the stops to get Kayla.

"When you have that look in your eye, it's usually one of two things—a business deal or a woman. Which is it?"

"It's both," Ethan answered. "I want Adams Cosmetics and I want Kayla Adams."

"Since when?" Daniel asked. "As I recall, Kayla had a thing for you when she was younger, but I would imagine her schoolgirl crush is over."

"I may not have given her the time of the day in the past, but I will now. And she is most definitely not a schoolgirl anymore," Ethan replied, "which means she's fair game." Back then, he'd had to turn her down, because it wouldn't have been right or legal, but now, there were no limits.

"So what are your plans?"

"Well, first I want you to place some calls and see how their quest to find potential investors is coming along, and then I want you to squash them. *I* want to be the only option, the only company that Adams Cosmetics can turn to."

"You mean the only man Kayla can turn to."

"That's one and the same."

"And how do you plan on breaking the ice between you and Ms. Adams?"

"I'm going to do what every man does when he's trying to woo a woman. I'm going to ask her out on a date," Ethan responded.

"I could kill you for the move you pulled at the premiere," Kayla told Piper, plopping down on the bed in her best friend's apartment after work. She'd arrived moments ago to help Piper pick out an outfit for her blind date after receiving an SOS text from Piper earlier that day.

"What move?" Piper asked innocently, even though she knew the move in question.

"You left me alone with Ethan Graham."

"And?" Piper raised a brow and glanced at Kayla as she held up a pantsuit. "What was wrong with that? Didn't you tell me years ago, after seeing the string of beautiful women Ethan dated, that you were over pining for him?"

"I know what I said. And I am not pining for him," Kayla replied testily. "And that suit is godawful. This is a date, not a business meeting." She snatched the ensemble out of Piper's hand and handed her another option. "Try this on."

Piper took the garment out of Kayla's hand and slid it

down her slender frame. "Are you saying you lied to your best friend of twenty years?" She held her chest as if crest-fallen.

"No," Kayla answered. She rose from the bed and zipped up the back of Piper's dress. "It's just that I thought I was over the man, but then…" Her voice trailed off as the image of Ethan's lips slowly starting to descend on hers came to mind.

Piper turned around. "But what?"

Kayla plopped back down on the bed and was silent. She hated to admit it, but she had no choice. "He still gets to me."

"Did something happen between you two when I left?"

Kayla nodded. "We almost kissed."

"What do you mean almost?" Piper asked. "You either did or you didn't."

"Well…we were interrupted because another couple burst onto the terrace," Kayla replied. "If they hadn't, I would have acted like a teenager and made out with the man. I can't be-lieve this, Piper." She jumped up. "Ethan was supposed to be in my past."

"Sounds like you two have some unfinished business," Piper mused. "Because clearly Ethan has tapped into some hidden desire you still have for him."

"No!" Kayla shook her head. "I refuse to give in to some teenage fantasy. I'm a grown woman who is capable of con-trolling her emotions, and I have to do that."

"Why?"

"Because…because I don't trust Ethan Graham one bit. He knows Adams Cosmetics is in trouble and he's ready to swoop in like the vulture his company is. I've heard what he's done to smaller companies that have merged with Graham International. I refuse to let Adams Cosmetics be a casualty."

"But don't you need the capital Ethan could provide?"

"I need capital, but there are other investors," Kayla replied. "And it's just a matter of time before I convince one of them to invest in Adams Cosmetics."

Kayla returned home to find the family had already gathered in the formal dining room for dinner.

"Kay, we didn't think you were joining us, so we started without you," her mother, Elizabeth, said as she entered.

"No worries, Mom." Kayla kissed her cheek before taking a seat at the table next to Shane.

"Where were you?" Courtney asked.

"I was at Piper's. She needed help choosing an outfit."

"I'm surprised Piper would need help in that department." Her father chuckled. "She seems to have a handle on...er... her personal sense of style."

That was her father's diplomatic way of saying Piper's taste bordered on eccentric, but that was okay with Kayla. They'd been best friends for twenty years and there was no one she trusted more.

"It's a blind date," Kayla offered. "And she wanted to make a good impression."

"You know I was surprised Andrew Jackson wasn't at the premiere," her father said. "He always did like a good show."

A silence came over the table, as the Jackson family was persona non grata in the Adams household.

"I ran into him last week," Kayla responded. "He was really interested in the fact that we were starting a new fragrance and mentioned that he just so happened to have been in France."

"The fragrance capital of the world." Shane rubbed his chin thoughtfully. Jackson could be up to something.

"Watch out for him," Byron said. "He's always been envious of our success."

"Oh, trust me, Daddy, I've got an eye on him at all times," Kayla said, laughing.

"That's good to hear. You'll need it," her mother said. "Anyway, you received a dozen calla lilies. They are on the table in the foyer."

"Really?" Kayla asked. She couldn't fathom who might have sent them. "From whom?"

"That's what we were wondering," Shane responded. "Do you have a secret admirer?"

Kayla rose from the table, but Victor was already on it and bringing her the card from the flowers. When had he sneaked out of the room? "Thank you, Victor."

"You're welcome," Victor said.

"So, who are they from?" Courtney inquired. "A new beau, perhaps?"

"Yeah, right. That's the last thing I need right now," Kayla said, pulling the card out of the envelope. She was surprised at the name on the card and had to read the message twice for fear she was hallucinating. The card stated, "Dinner. Tomorrow at 7:00 p.m. Will pick you up. Ethan."

Why was Ethan sending her flowers? And did he think he could just order her to dinner and she would comply? "Anyway, it's no one important." She placed the card back in the envelope and slid it inside her purse.

"Hmm…if it's no one important, you should tell us," Shane said from her side.

Kayla glared at Shane before rising from the table. "Umm, I don't think I'm hungry after all." She grabbed her purse. "I'll see you all later." She quickly rushed out of the room. She had business to attend to, namely, setting Ethan Graham straight.

* * *

Ethan had just prepared himself an after-dinner cocktail and was relaxing in his living room when his doorbell rang. He had a loft in the city, but after living abroad the past few years while expanding Graham International, he much preferred his nine-bedroom, nine-bath mansion in Tuxedo Park.

He answered the door himself because he'd told the staff they could retire for the evening. So not only was the visitor shocked to see him answer the door, but he was equally shocked to see her. "Kayla!"

"Ethan." Kayla pushed past him into the foyer. "I need to talk to you." She stood in the hallway, then began pacing back and forth.

Ethan smiled. She must have received his flowers, and if the furious expression on Kayla's face was any indication, she was not happy about it. "And this couldn't wait until our dinner tomorrow night?"

"No."

"Well, then, by all means let's talk." He motioned with his arm for Kayla to follow him. He led her down the hall to the study where he'd been reading.

Once in the study, Kayla let him have it. "You have no right to send me a summons."

"A summons?" Ethan's brow rose. "I believe you're mistaken. It was an invitation to dinner."

Kayla pulled the envelope from her purse. "This was not an invitation because you did not expect to be turned down."

Ethan sat down with his decanter in hand and folded one leg over the other. He sipped before speaking. "And I presume you are here at this hour—" he looked at his Movado watch and it read eight o'clock "—to decline my invitation."

"I will not be ordered around, especially by you."

Ethan's mouth formed an O. "Especially by me. Why is

that, Kayla? What do you have against me? Correct me if I'm wrong—" he rubbed his beard thoughtfully "—but had we not been interrupted the other night, you and I would have finally shared that long-awaited kiss you've always wanted. So what exactly is so abhorrent about sharing dinner with me?"

"You're wrong!" Kayla responded even though her face turned several shades of red.

"Am I?" Ethan rose from the chair. "I think it's time we find out exactly what's between us. Don't you?"

Kayla took a step back. "I wouldn't share a meal with you if I was dying of hunger."

Ethan chuckled. "Well, fortunately, you're not."

"Which is why I'm declining."

"I refuse to take no for an answer."

"You may not be used to hearing the word *no,* Ethan, but I meant what I said the other night. I want no part of you or your company."

"Those are mighty big words for a woman in a bind. I would think you'd be chomping at the bit to pitch your investment strategy to me personally, as I am Graham International."

"I have been looking after my family's company for a long time, Ethan, and I most certainly don't need you to bail me out."

Ethan placed the decanter on a side table and walked toward her. Kayla stood up ramrod straight. She refused to be bullied by Ethan and was determined to stand up to him, even though butterflies were jumping around in her stomach at his nearness. She took a deep breath and calmed herself.

"No, I don't imagine you need me just yet." Ethan's fierce brown eyes focused on hers, and Kayla found she couldn't turn away from his piercing gaze that was drenched with hunger. "But you want me."

Kayla swallowed hard.

"Oh, yes." He watched Kayla nervously look downward. "You want me, but you're afraid to show it. But that's all right, I have no problem going for what I want." Ethan grabbed Kayla by the shoulders and his mouth slammed down on hers, stealing her breath and fracturing her thoughts into a million pieces. Before she knew what was happening, he had her up against the bookshelves and was pressing his body against her. He cupped the back of her head as his mouth kissed her with fervor.

Kayla was unprepared for the onslaught of Ethan's mouth on hers or the rush of excitement that coursed through her. She'd thought the kiss would be hard and fast but instead his lips were surprisingly gentle and soft as they searched hers. His tongue traced the outline of her lips and despite herself, she parted them, allowing him entry. His tongue slipped inside and he began plundering the inner recesses of her mouth. The kiss sent the pit of her stomach swirling and caused spirals of ecstasy to shoot straight through her. When he began sucking on her tongue voraciously, drawing her to him, Kayla gripped his arms and a moan escaped from her.

Ethan didn't stop at kissing her. His hands were everywhere, touching her, caressing her breasts over her trench coat and cupping her bottom firmly against him as he deepened the kiss, fusing their two tongues as one. He tantalized and teased her equally, leaving her weak with need.

It was a slow, drugging kiss and when it was over, Kayla was shocked by her eager response. She dragged her mouth away from his and stepped away, embarrassed by her own wantonness. Was he right? Had she been waiting, wanting this all along? Her heart was pounding and her body ached for fulfillment. What was wrong with her? Her senses were reeling as if short-circuited.

"Now that was a proper kiss," Ethan said. "And long overdue."

His response snapped Kayla out of her kiss-induced daze. "You just had to put your foot in your mouth, didn't you?" He'd broken the intimate moment between them and made Kayla realize just how close she'd come to losing control. She reached for her purse that had somehow fallen on the floor in the kiss and headed toward the door.

"Where are you going?" Ethan asked.

Kayla spun around. "Did you think that the next logical step was for us to go upstairs to bed? Because if so, you were dead wrong. The kiss was pleasant enough, but if you think it's enough to render me free of my faculties, then you had better think again. I am not easily seduced, either out of my clothes or out of my company. Consider this your notice that I am declining your invitation to dinner. Have a good night." Kayla stalked out of the room with as much dignity as was possible after she'd so easily succumbed to his charms.

On the other side of the wall, Ethan was stunned. Kayla Adams was a spitfire. And he loved it. She'd set his body ablaze, which was why a certain member was straining in his trousers.

He'd only meant to have a little taste, but instead her full lips had released a passion that had been lying dormant, and her well-defined rear end had him horny as hell. He could only imagine what it would be like to make love to such a siren. Kayla was like a wild Arabian horse. But he would look forward to riding her, because to tame her would be no fun at all.

Tonight, she'd shown her hand. That kiss had told him everything he needed to know. Kayla wanted him as much as he wanted her, but she would not come to him of her own accord. She was determined to show she was unaffected, which meant he was going to have to up the seduction.

An idea suddenly began to form in his head. He'd secretly wanted Kayla for years, but the rift in their families had never given him a chance to spend much time with her. But the more he saw of her now, the more convinced he became that she was what he'd always been looking for. He was well overdue to settle down and start a family. He needed a woman by his side who would complement him, who understood the business but was passionate enough in the bedroom to make him forget about it. A woman he could respect and who would be an excellent mother to his children. A woman who was beautiful yet confident, strong, intelligent, stubborn and sexy as hell. Kayla Adams fit the bill perfectly. If this idea came to fruition, he could have Kayla and correct the mistake Carter had made years ago with Byron. Kayla would hate him for it, but Ethan had a proposition for her. One she wouldn't be able to turn down if she wanted to save her family's company.

Chapter 4

Kayla was still lying in the bed the next morning and it was well after seven. She knew she should be getting ready for work, but how could she? She'd slept fitfully the night before. Visions of Ethan and the sudden surge of lust he'd evoked had kept her awake.

She told herself it was just curiosity from finally having the object of her teenage infatuation. Or maybe it was because it had been a long time since a man had roused that kind of passion in her. But she knew better. The sexual chemistry between them was so strong it had consumed her and shattered her resolve to keep him at bay. She was furious with her body's betrayal. In the cold light of day, it was impossible to ignore that every part of her had wanted Ethan last night. The question was, what was she going to do about it?

Kayla was anxious. The prospectus listing the shares of Adams Cosmetics had gone out confidentially to several private investors and companies, but it had been over a week and she hadn't heard a thing. She was beginning to worry that their company could be going up in smoke when her assistant, Myra, poked her head in the door.

"Kayla, are you free?"

Kayla smiled warmly at Myra. She had come a long way in the past two years. She'd started out as a mousy mess, but now after working with Kayla she was poised and confident and had no problem calling her by her first name. "Yes, what is it?"

"Ethan Graham is here to see you."

"Excuse me?" Kayla's head popped up from the file she was reading. She hadn't expected to hear that name so soon, especially after their encounter last night. Sure, she suspected they would reconnect at some point, but not so soon.

"Umm, umm," Kayla stammered and began shuffling the file around to close it. Myra stared back at her, clearly stunned to see her boss at a loss for words. "Tell him I'll be with him in a minute."

"There will be no minute," Ethan said from the door of her office. "We'll talk now."

Kayla's eyes rose to meet his and when she did, she inhaled sharply. Ethan's mesmerizingly dark, deep-set eyes, the ones she'd gotten lost in as a naive young girl, were directly on her.

"Kayla." Ethan walked toward her, commanding her absolute attention from his six-foot-three presence.

Kayla managed to tear her eyes away from Ethan for a second to tell her starstruck assistant, who was also staring at Ethan, "That will be all, thank you."

"Ethan." Since they were in a professional setting, Kayla offered her hand as she rose, which Ethan shook.

"You're looking good," Ethan stated, standing back to

admire her in the two-piece navy suit she was wearing. It was completely professional, showing little of what he knew to be a curvy body underneath all those clothes.

"Ethan!"

"I don't believe in wasting time," Ethan returned as he sat across from her. "I believe in getting down to business."

"And you think I'm your business?"

"Not yet, but you will be," Ethan responded. "I'm here to discuss Adams Cosmetics."

"I told you I was not interested in Graham International as a potential investor," she countered icily.

"I think that would be a grave mistake. Why don't you try treating me as you would any other investor? You might be surprised at what I have to offer you."

"Fine." She sighed. She was tired of fighting. "Have a seat." She motioned to the chair in front of her large executive desk. "All right," Kayla said, folding her arms across her chest. "Well, we have some great projects in the pipeline, but have run short of capital, as I'm sure you're aware. If you'd like, I can contact Shane and bring him in to discuss some of the plans we have." Kayla reached for the phone on her desk, but Ethan placed his large masculine hand over hers. His touch sent a tingling sensation shooting right through her core and she pulled her hand away suddenly.

"I don't need Shane," Ethan returned. "I only need you." Kayla was chattering endlessly because he'd caught her off-guard, which was good. She wouldn't expect what was coming next.

Kayla swallowed hard and suddenly became uncomfortable. Ethan was looking at her with the same intent gaze he'd had last night before he'd kissed her.

"What is it that you want, Ethan?"

"I want what you offered me seventeen years ago but I couldn't collect on then."

Kayla laughed falsely. "What *are* you talking about?"

Ethan smiled broadly, revealing a set of perfect white teeth behind his large succulent lips. "You know what I'm talking about." He stared her directly in the eye and watched Kayla's cheeks burn in acknowledgment of the memory.

"Are you kidding me? I was young and clearly out of mind when I came on to you. And I can't believe you would dare to bring that up."

Ethan popped out of his seat to lean across the desk. He gave her body a raking gaze. "I've been wanting you since that day, and we both know I'm used to getting what I want."

Kayla's eyes narrowed and she smirked. "Yes, we do."

"You were too young for me to act on our mutual attraction, but we're both adults now…"

Understanding started to dawn on Kayla. "Oh, I see, in exchange for a romp in the sack with me, you'll invest in Adams Cosmetics. Get out of my office!"

Kayla hurried to the door to show him out, but with long purposeful strides, Ethan reached her in no time and grabbed her arm. "I'm offering you a darn good deal. Not only do you get me, but Graham International will pour millions into Adams Cosmetics and save it from bankruptcy."

"There are no limits to your audacity, are there?" She snatched her arm away. "You have no right to come into my office, manhandle me and demand I sleep with you or else you won't invest in my company. It's despicable."

"I have every right." Ethan stepped closer to her and Kayla could smell his musky masculine scent. "You want a great deal of money to save this sinking ship, and it comes with a price."

"Sleep with you or else?"

"No," Ethan returned. "Marry me or else."

Shane burst through her office door seconds later. "Sis, I heard Ethan Graham is in the building—" He stopped short, blinking in bafflement that he'd clearly interrupted a moment.

Ethan walked toward him and shook Shane's hand warmly. "Shane, it's good to see you again."

"You, as well," Shane responded and glanced over at his sister. "Kay, are you okay?" he asked, because all color had gone out of her face.

"I...I..." Kayla glanced at Ethan's smug face and then back at her brother. She was experiencing a gamut of perplexing emotions. "I...I need a glass of water." With leaden feet, she walked over to her wet bar and with trembling hands opened a bottled water. Marry Ethan or else? What the hell was he thinking? He was the last person she wanted to marry.

She brought the bottle to her lips and turned to face them.

"Are you here to talk about investing?" Shane inquired.

"More or less," Ethan glanced at Kayla, whom he'd struck into silence with his bold offer. He'd thought long and hard and realized that Kayla was the only woman he'd ever known who shared his love of money and thrived on power. He'd spent years searching for someone who could hold her own with him, when Kayla had been that someone all along.

"That's great!" Shane said enthusiastically. "I'd be happy to show what I'm working on in the lab, if you're interested."

"Absolutely," Ethan responded. With fluid strides he strode to the door with Shane, but stopped short. "Kayla, we'll finish our discussion when I get back."

Kayla rolled her eyes. There was no discussion. He was

giving her an ultimatum. Marry him or risk losing her family business.

Ethan returned nearly an hour later and Kayla was no more ready for him than when he'd left. In fact, she was offended that he would think she was for sale.

"Have you thought about my offer?" Ethan inquired. He strolled to her chair and whirled her around to face him.

"Your offer? Is that what you would call it?" Kayla hissed.

"I think it's very reasonable," Ethan responded to her hostile tone. "In exchange for my investing millions in this company and putting my reputation on the line, you marry me. I see it as a win-win for the both of us. You get the capital you need and I get a sexy wife out of the arrangement."

Kayla wasn't about to let the compliment trip her up. "Your offer is far from reasonable. It's disgusting."

Ethan raised a brow. "Really? I didn't feel your disgust when I was kissing you last night. In fact, I felt you come alive at my touch." He leaned down and brushed his fingertips across her arm on the chair. "Come on, Kayla, don't you think it's time we finally explored the sexual tension that's underneath the surface? Think about how much fun we'll have exploring each other's bodies." He caressed her cheek softly.

Kayla was floored by the way he was speaking to her. No other man would have dared speak to her in such a manner, but then again, Ethan was like no other man she'd known. Was that why she could never let another man get close, because she was still holding on to the hope of one day having Ethan? She shook her head and quickly dismissed the idea. He was just tapping into some hidden desires because she'd been celibate for some time.

"Stop touching me." Kayla moved away from him, her pulse spinning, and looked out of the window. "You're trying to confuse me." She was swimming through a haze of anger and desire.

"I'm not trying to confuse you, Kayla," Ethan whispered softly in her ear as he came to stand next her. "I thought I was being quite clear. Marrying me will solidify this company and our families. Think about the power we'd have. We'd own this town. And I've always been part of the Adams family anyway, except now it'll be official."

"You think this is so cut-and-dried and tidy. Marry you and that's it?" Kayla asked, facing him. "How do you know that I don't have a man? And that I'm not sharing someone else's bed?"

Ethan frowned. The report had been clear, Kayla was currently single. Had his investigator gotten it wrong? Kayla was his now, and he'd didn't want any complications. "If you were sharing someone else's bed, I doubt you would have responded to me as you did, but it doesn't matter because it's over now," Ethan responded. "You're mine."

The smoldering flame she saw in his eyes startled her. "I am not something you can take possession of, Ethan Graham," Kayla replied. "And there are other investors out there, so you can take your offer and shove it."

"Those are bold words for someone who's running out of options," Ethan said. "But I can see that this has come as a shock to you, so I will give you some time to think over my offer. But trust me when I say that there is no escaping the inevitable, as I intend to have you, Kayla Adams."

A short while later, after she'd had time to stop quivering with fury, Kayla went to Shane's lab. "Can I come in?" Kayla asked, popping her head inside. She needed a dose of reality. What Ethan had proposed was ludicrous. She couldn't possibly marry him.

"Of course. Has Ethan gone?" Shane asked as he fiddled with several vials on the counter that were cooling. He'd just finished heating up raw extracts of sandalwood, jasmine and vanilla to remove the essential oils. He needed the right combination of base, middle and top notes for the new fragrance.

"Yes, thank God!" Kayla jumped onto the stool across from Shane. She loved being in the lab with all the bottles lined up in tiered rows on Shane's perfumer's organ and watching him experiment with new oils and scents. She'd been terrible at chemistry, but Shane had always excelled. He had a special gift for making something out of nothing.

Shane stared at Kayla. "Are you okay, sis?"

"Yeah, I'm fine."

"You don't seem fine," he responded. "Earlier, when Ethan was here, you looked really tense. And it looked like I walked in on something between you two. Did he say or do something to offend you?"

How about suggest marrying him and handing over our family business? Kayla couldn't tell Shane everything he'd said, so she told him a version of it. "That I'm on a sinking ship?" Kayla laughed bitterly. "Then yes."

"He said that?"

"Oh, yes." Kayla nodded. "He thinks he's our greatest hope."

"Did you tell him we're looking at other investors?"

"Of course, but the man has a humongous ego."

Shane stopped working and walked over to Kayla. He picked up both her hands. "True, but I can see that you're worried."

"I don't want to lose Daddy's life's work. I would do anything to save it."

Shane didn't like the desperate sound in his sister's voice.

"Well, hopefully, it won't come down to that. Michael will find us an investor." He squeezed her hand before letting go and walking back to the concoction he was working on.

"I hope so."

"I noticed how you avoided my first comment."

"Which was?"

"That I interrupted an intimate moment between you and Ethan."

Kayla scooted off the stool and picked up a vial to smell the scent. She was anxious about the question her brother was posing. "Smells good, but I don't know what you're talking about."

"Oh, yes, you do," Shane said, pulling the vial out of her hands and placing it back in the holder. "Do you still have the hots for Ethan?"

Kayla laughed. "The hots. Shane, seriously?"

"Oh, c'mon, Kayla. Don't act like it was my imagination. I may be two years younger than you, but I remember how you used to moon over Ethan every time he came around."

"I did not."

Shane smiled. "Did, too."

"Well, you don't have worry, Shane. I am no longer carrying a torch for Ethan Graham."

"If you say so, sis."

And she did. Or at least she hoped she did.

A week later, Kayla was frustrated. One investor had canceled their meeting at the last minute with no plausible explanation. Another had agreed to a meeting, but, one expensive lunch later, had expressed that Adams Cosmetics was too much of a risk for him and had bowed out. Kayla threw her stapler across the room. It landed with a thud by the door.

Her assistant, Myra, came rushing inside. "Is everything okay, Kayla?" Concern was etched over her round face as she picked up the stapler and set it back on Kayla's desk.

"Everything is fine, Myra. Sorry about that."

"No problem. Let me know if you need anything."

Kayla nodded. As Myra was leaving, Michael came in and closed the door behind him. He sat in the chair across from her with a glum look.

"Today did not go as I'd planned."

"Ya think?" Kayla asked sarcastically. "Did word of our meeting somehow leak? Do you think the Jacksons had anything to do with this?" She didn't trust Andrew or his stepdaughter, Monica, and knew they would be circling like vultures looking for a sign of weakness.

"Of course not," Michael replied. "I had each investor sign a confidentiality agreement. I'm sorry, Kayla, he did seem like a viable candidate."

Kayla ran her fingers through her curls. "I'm sorry, too, Michael. I didn't mean to bite your head off. I know you are doing your best. I'm just a little on edge."

"Trust me, I know." She'd been riding Michael for weeks about investors. For some reason, it seemed more urgent than ever before for Kayla. "But we have another meeting scheduled for next week. And there's one other elusive investor out of Germany that I'm tracking down for a meeting. We may be down, but we're not out yet."

"Thank you, Michael." Kayla gave a tentative smile. She needed a pick-me-up talk, because otherwise she might have to give Ethan's offer serious thought, and that was a frightening prospect.

On a Saturday in mid-April, Kayla prepared to join her family for the annual ritual of attending the horse race at Atlanta Steeplechase, which benefited the Starlight Children's Foundation of Georgia and the University of Georgia's College of Veterinary Medicine.

Kayla was putting on her finest spring attire to attend the outdoor event. There would be a fabulous picnic in the picnic box space they owned, all prearranged by Victor, who would be attending the event to ensure everything went smoothly. And of course, there was the hat contest.

Kayla, Courtney and their mother had already gone shopping for just the right hat for the event, as everyone knew it was all about who had the most fashionable hat. Kayla couldn't care less about horse racing, but it was a chance to schmooze with the Atlanta elite and be seen. The business community had to know Adams Cosmetics was here to stay.

A knock sounded on Kayla's bedroom door. "Come in!"

It was her mother and Courtney, both holding hatboxes. "We've brought gifts!" Her mother held up a box.

"I presume that is mine?" Kayla inquired, pulling a large-brimmed black-and-white straw hat with a big bow and ribbon out of a box. She'd had no time to shop for one. Thankfully, it matched the black-and-white plaid strapless dress she was wearing. Kayla put the hat over her hair, which was in a simple ponytail, and admired herself in the pedestal mirror.

"Sure is," Courtney answered, coming to stand behind her in the mirror. "It's just as audacious as this one." She pulled out a strange hat which had some type of colorful bird pinned on it and looked like it was about to take flight. "I have to win the hat contest."

"You just may." Kayla laughed. "Are you participating in the fashion show again this year?"

"Duh, of course I am." Courtney relished being center-stage, and what better opportunity than being onstage surrounded by admirers? "Guess who I heard is going to be there?"

Kayla took the bait and glanced behind her. "Who?"

"Ethan Graham." Courtney smiled devilishly at her sister.

"Don't tell your father that," their mother said. "You know how he feels about Ethan."

"I don't understand why there's bad blood between him and Ethan. Ethan never did anything to Daddy," Courtney replied.

"You were too young to remember," Kayla said, "but Ethan once offered Daddy money to sell Adams Cosmetics."

"He did?"

"Yes, he did," their mother answered. "And your father turned him down flat. The move was something that Carter would have done and was completely out of character for Ethan. I always thought he did it to please Carter. Your father, on the other hand, never forgot. He's been happy that Ethan has been abroad, but now…"

"I will take care of Ethan." Kayla patted her mother's arm.

Courtney raised a brow. "Oh, you will?"

"Yes." Kayla glared at her sister. "Are you ready to go, Mom?"

"Yes, dear. Let me just go check with your father."

Twenty minutes later they were seated in the limo for the hour-and-a-half ride out of Atlanta. Victor had already left an hour prior to go to prepare the picnic boxes with tents. They filled their time on the ride talking about what else but Adams Cosmetics. Shane discussed the mixture of scents he was working on and Courtney regaled them with a story on her last press event for the company.

Kayla spent the time on the drive wondering how she was going to handle Ethan. He wasn't going to take no for an answer. He was going to try to wear her down and make her see things his way, but Kayla refused to be bullied. Or forced into marrying a man she didn't love or who didn't love her. All he wanted was her in his bed. Was sex with her really worth all he would be giving up? His freedom? His bachelorhood? Or perhaps he intended to continue his lifestyle after he'd married her?

"Are you okay?" her father asked from her side as she stared blankly out the window. "You've been awfully quiet."

"I'm okay, Daddy," she fibbed. "Just have a lot on my mind."

"Everything will work out, baby girl." He gave her shoulders a gentle squeeze.

If only things were that easy, thought Kayla.

The weather was sunny and bright when they arrived at the Kingston Downs Race Course in Rome, Georgia. The limo dropped them off a distance from their picnic box on the hillside and they had to walk the rest of the way. Kayla had worn sensible shoes, unlike Courtney, who was doing a darn good job of walking in her four-inch strappy sandals.

When they arrived at their box, Victor had already decorated their tables with fine linens, crystal and cutlery. A beautiful floral centerpiece decorated each table. Her mother had invited several top-level Adams executives and their spouses to the event. "You've outdone yourself, Victor," her mother gushed, kissing him on the cheek.

"You're welcome, Mrs. Adams. Would anyone care for some champagne?" Victor inquired.

"Would love some, Vic," her father said.

While Victor took the liberty of filling everyone's flutes, Kayla looked around nervously, wringing her hands. The Graham picnic box neighbored theirs because their father had purchased them at the same time. It was supposed to be an annual event for both families to enjoy, but over the years, it had turned into a test of wills on who could go the longest without speaking. Of course, once Carter had passed away, tensions had eased as Ethan rarely came to the event, except this year. Kayla was certain Ethan was nearby.

"You seem quite chipper today," Daniel said to Ethan as they walked around the track, speaking to several business colleagues at the Atlanta Steeplechase event.

"Oh, yes." Ethan smiled. "I'm quite pleased with an idea I had recently."

"Care to fill me in? Or is it a secret?"

Ethan turned to Daniel and his mouth curved into an unconscious smile. "I can't say just yet, but if you've done your job all the pieces will be in place soon."

"What job are you referring to?"

"I asked you to squash any other investment deal that Adams Cosmetics might encounter."

"It's a work in progress," Daniel stated. Ethan pursed his lips and Daniel knew that was his way of saying he didn't like his comment. "I have to tread carefully, Ethan. You don't want word of this leaking out."

"True."

"I've already convinced two other investors that they should consider investing in Graham International, a sure bet."

"Wonderful. Keep up the good work."

"In the meantime, I'm going to go stoke the fire," Ethan said, heading back toward his picnic box, but then it occurred to him that Byron Adams would not be too pleased to see him. He would have to sidestep Kayla's old man to get some alone time with her. So where else would he find her? The answer came to him clear as day.

Chapter 5

"Kayla, did you hear what I said?" Courtney repeated herself.

Kayla blinked several times. She was preoccupied looking across the field for some sign of Ethan. "Hmm…what was that?"

"I asked if you wanted to go to the stables to look at the horses."

"Oh, sure," Kayla answered. She'd always loved riding and competing. This was just the thing she needed to get her mind off Ethan. She was wound up like a knot waiting for Ethan to make his presence known and it was driving her crazy.

The two of them made their way through the crowd to the stables to look at the beautiful animals. The stables were filled with jockeys, their families and general spectators.

No sooner had they arrived than Courtney abandoned her in favor of a hottie she saw in the stables, so Kayla took the time to get her head together. She found a prize beauty of a horse, a beautiful chestnut Arabian mare that was chomping at the bit. Kayla loved her long lean body, large eyes and high-carriage tail.

"May I?" Kayla asked the jockey, and when he nodded, she took the liberty of grabbing the brush off the nearby hook and brushing the thoroughbred's shiny chestnut coat. "She's beautiful," Kayla commented to the jockey.

"Yeah, but she's a handful."

"Beautiful things usually are," another masculine voice said from behind her.

Kayla didn't have to turn around to know the owner of that voice. He'd found her. Kayla glanced sideways at him. "Ethan."

"How did I know I'd find you here?" Ethan said, smiling as he strolled toward her.

Kayla didn't answer. Instead, she just talked softly to the horse and fed him a carrot.

"Boy, do I wish I was that horse," Ethan said as he stood watching her. When the jockey stepped away, he whispered in her ear, "I would love to have you stroke me gently."

Kayla stiffened and stopped brushing the horse. "Must you equate everything to sex?"

Ethan laughed heartily. "It's funny, but when I'm around you that's all I seem to think about," he admitted.

"Well, keep it clean." Kayla returned. "There are children around." She nodded to the children around them in the stables.

"Of course," Ethan responded, glancing around him. "Have you given my offer any more thought?"

Kayla leaned around him to put the brush back on the hook. "No, I haven't." She turned and started walking toward the entrance. Ethan fell in step with her.

"Don't you think you should? Time is running out."

Kayla stopped short. "I didn't recall that I had a time limit on my answer."

Just then, a bell rang in the distance, signaling the races would begin soon. Everyone began to disperse as the jockeys began ushering the horses out onto the grass. Kayla started toward the exit, but Ethan grabbed her arm.

"Not so fast." He spun Kayla around into the nearest empty stall.

"What do you think you're doing?" Kayla asked when Ethan backed her up against the stall and put his hands on either side of her face.

"Reminding you of what's between us." He lowered his head and started nuzzling her neck. He took little nibbles at her neck and then his tongue began a hot trail all the way up to her ear. He flicked his tongue back and forth across one ear, teasing her into submission. Kayla pushed against his rock-hard chest, but it was useless, she could feel her guard collapsing. The prolonged anticipation of having Ethan's lips on hers was unbearable. Her stomach began to quiver and her heart began to thunder loudly in her chest.

Ethan made his way to her face, kissing her forehead and her cheeks before landing on her mouth. Oh, yes, the luscious mouth he'd spent the last week dying to taste. He explored her mouth thoroughly, sampling and devouring all at once. He ravished her mouth while his hands moved gently down the length of her back, reveling in her curves until she floated weightless in his arms. His hands explored her waist and her hips before cupping her backside to press her more firmly against him. She kissed him back with a hunger that belied her earlier calm.

"Ahem." A cough from the stable door caused them both to look up. It was Courtney.

"Uh…" For once Courtney was too stunned to speak. She blinked several times at the shock of finding Kayla and Ethan in each other's arms. "Uh…I…I was looking for you."

"Well…I…I'm here," Kayla panted breathlessly. Chest heaving, she stepped out of Ethan's arms, smoothed down her dress and walked toward her sister. "Let's go."

Ethan smiled to himself as the women departed. He was breaking down all of Kayla's defenses, and with any luck, he'd finally be able to have her.

"What the heck was going on back there?" Courtney asked once they were no longer in earshot of the stables.

"I don't want to talk about it." Kayla looked straight ahead. She felt like a breathless girl of seventeen and it scared her.

"Oh, that is not going to fly, big sis," Courtney returned. "It's not every day I find you making out with the object of your affection."

"You are making too much of this."

"Are you kidding me?" Courtney laughed from her side. "Matter of fact, I think Daddy would love to hear about you and Ethan's newfound romance."

That stopped Kayla dead in her tracks and she spun around. "You wouldn't dare!"

"I will if you don't spill the beans."

"That's blackmail."

Courtney bunched her shoulders.

"Fine." Kayla sighed. She would tell Courtney the least amount of information as possible. There was no reason for her to know Ethan's true motives or what she might have to do to save the family company. "Since Ethan returned, we recently started seeing each other." It was part truth and part fiction. They weren't really *dating,* but she needed to satisfy her sister's curiosity.

"And those flowers last week. Were they from him?"

Kayla nodded. "Please don't tell Daddy. You know how he feels about Ethan."

"I do," Courtney said. "But I also know you've been harboring a crush on Ethan for a very long time. It must be pretty thrilling to finally *be* with him." She smiled knowingly.

"Courtney!" Kayla's cheeks colored. "Things have not gone that far."

"But wouldn't you like them to?" Courtney winked.

Her sister was incorrigible. "Do we have to continue this conversation?" Kayla rolled her eyes upward.

"No, we don't." Courtney smiled brightly and continued walking toward their picnic box. "You are no fun, Kay."

Kayla followed behind her. "I like my privacy."

"I won't tell Daddy a word," Courtney responded. "Scouts honor." She turned around and held up two fingers as she walked backward. Kayla could only hope Courtney would keep her word. Otherwise, their father would blow a gasket.

By the end of the following week, after another failed meeting with an investor, Kayla was at her wit's end. She was running out of options. What was she going to do? Today, she had her final meeting with Rupert Martin, a German investor who was known for taking risks. She was holding out hope that this meeting would be what they needed to get them back in the black.

Kayla stared out the window of the Adams Cosmetics building. If this meeting failed, she would be forced to seriously consider Ethan's marriage proposal.

Kayla made her way to the boardroom and found Shane and Courtney had already arrived. This time she'd brought reinforcements. They would both sit in on the meeting, as they realized just how important this investor was to the company's existence. Shane had prepared prototypes of the perfume bottles and had test samples of his latest fragrance creation for the investor to sample.

"Are you okay?" Shane asked when she walked in and concern was etched across her face. "You're looking a bit tense."

Kayla pulled Shane aside. "You and I both know that this is the last meeting Michael has set up."

"True, but Rupert Martin is not the only investor. Michael went after the top four, but there are others out there."

"Not who can come up with the kind of cash we are looking for as quickly as we need."

"Don't lose faith, Kayla." Shane squeezed her shoulder.

Kayla nodded, but she knew better. Adams Cosmetics was hemorrhaging money at an alarming rate and if they didn't stop the bleeding soon, they would no longer be able to operate.

"Today is the day, yes?" Ethan asked Daniel in his office.

"Yes," Daniel stated. "Adams Cosmetics' meeting with Rupert Martin is this afternoon."

"He's the last one."

Daniel nodded. "Rupert felt he owed her the courtesy of at least hearing her offer before making his final decision, but I feel it's a moot point. After he turns her down, Kayla will have no choice but to take your offer of 51 percent ownership. Adams Cosmetics will be yours."

Ethan leaned back in his chair. Adams Cosmetics would fit nicely with Graham International and shore up his cosmetics division, which despite all the high-level executives he'd brought in had never quite lived up to its potential once Byron Adams started his own company. It's why he'd focused his attention on the clothing and leather goods division.

"Good. Have my car brought around. I'm going to the Adams Cosmetics offices." The AC offices were in downtown Atlanta, just a few blocks from Graham International's corporate headquarters. He knew he was just a short ride away from victory.

"Do you think that's wise?" Daniel asked. "They'll be licking their wounds after today's meeting."

"Which is precisely the reason to strike now."

Daniel was amazed at Ethan's cutthroat tactics, but what could he expect from a man who was slowly developing a reputation as a corporate raider?

An hour later, Rupert Martin had turned them down. Graciously, but turned them down nonetheless. Kayla watched Shane sit slumped down in his chair. Even Courtney was surprisingly quiet and stared blankly at the wall. They all knew that the end was near. As Michael walked Rupert Martin out, Kayla made one last-ditch effort.

She rushed out of the boardroom and met the men at the elevator. "Rupert, I would love a private word with you." He'd insisted she call him by his first name during the meeting.

"Ms. Adams, I really must be going."

"Five minutes." Kayla held up one hand. She was hoping he'd give her a second chance to plead her case.

"Very well. Lead the way."

Kayla led Rupert to her office. She noticed Michael's imploring eyes wondering what she was up to, but Kayla had no time. She had to react. She closed her door and came to sit beside Rupert who sat in the chair opposite her desk.

"I won't waste your time," Kayla said. "I'll get right to

the point. I know we've asked you to take a significant risk in investing in Adams Cosmetics, but I'm prepared to offer you an incentive."

Rupert's ear perked up. "I'm listening."

"In exchange for your investment, I am prepared to sell you half of my shares. Adding my 12.5 shares to the 37.5 already on the table would give you a 50 percent ownership stake of Adams Cosmetics. We would be your partner."

"Like hell you will," a masculine voice said from the doorway.

Kayla looked up and saw Ethan towering in her doorway. He stormed toward them with a look of fury in his eyes that scared Kayla, and she literally jumped out of her seat.

Ethan stood in front of them. He was determined to thwart Kayla's meeting and seize his chance to right what his father had done wrong with Graham International years ago. If Carter had been willing to compromise with Byron and give him more say in the company operations, they would never have lost their highest-grossing division. Today, he could bring Adams Cosmetics back into the fold where it belonged. And finally have a real chance with the woman who had eluded him for years.

"Rupert, you will have to forgive Ms. Adams," Ethan said. "She had no idea that I'd put in this offer to her board." He pulled out a slip of paper and held it out for Rupert to read.

"What offer?" Kayla asked. "Rupert, please listen to me. We can make this deal."

But Rupert ignored her and spoke directly to Ethan. "Mr. Graham." He returned the sheet of paper to Ethan. "That is quite a substantial offer and one I could not come close to meeting, even with 50 percent ownership." He turned to Kayla. "Ms. Adams, best of luck to you in your new venture." He nodded at Ethan before closing the door to her office.

"Ohmigod, do you have any idea what you've done?" Kayla cried. "You've just killed the last opportunity of saving my father's company." She fell backward into her chair. Her head fell to her hands and she began sobbing.

Ethan hated to see Kayla so upset, but he had no other choice. He bent down until he was inches away from her face. "You have one opportunity remaining, Kayla. Mine."

Kayla glanced up at Ethan and saw red. "I hate you!" she yelled and rose from her chair.

"Kayla, please, you're upset," Ethan said. "And I understand why, but trust me when I say that this is for the best. Could you honestly have given up half your company to an outsider because you don't want to merge with GI? Sign over *thirteen* of your shares to me, and as my wife, Adams Cosmetics will remain in the family."

"I said get away from me!" Kayla yelled louder so Ethan would get the hint.

Ethan held up his hands and rose. "Okay, okay. I will leave for now, but I want you at my house *tonight*. I want this finalized by the end of the day."

"Out!" She pointed to the door. As Ethan walked to the door, Kayla followed him, and he was barely out before she slammed the door and crumpled against it.

Kayla sat in her Porsche Carrera outside of Ethan's estate. She was trying to decide if she wanted to race off the grounds and test out her Porche's max speed limit of 205 mph. Because today had been the day from hell. After Ethan had left, Shane and Courtney had both come to her office to discuss the meetings, but she'd refused to see them. How could she look at them knowing she'd let them down?

She was supposed to be their big sister. She was supposed to take care of them, but she'd failed miserably.

And so she'd paced in her office for hours after everyone left until finally deciding to meet Ethan at his estate, if only to turn him down to his face. She would rather close Adams Cosmetics' doors than give in to him.

Ethan looked through the foyer curtain. Kayla had been sitting in her car for nearly half an hour. It was time he ended it, so he opened his front door and walked outside in the cool spring evening. He knocked on the driver's window.

Kayla rolled down the window. "Yes?"

"Do you plan on staying out here all night?" Ethan inquired. "Or do you plan on coming in anytime soon?"

That was the very question she'd been debating the entire time. After several moments, Kayla rolled up the window, took a deep breath and stepped out of the vehicle.

"Thank you." Ethan closed the door behind her.

Kayla strode in front of him without looking back, but Ethan didn't have a problem with it. He was enjoying the view of her rear end in the jeans she wore. As they entered the foyer, Ethan noticed she'd dressed casually in a fitted white top that ruched at the sides and a pair of skinny jeans. If she thought the effect would lessen how sexy she was to him, she was mistaken. He was even more aroused.

"Would you like a drink?" Ethan asked, closing the front door behind him.

"I could use a vodka straight up." She followed Ethan into the great room and watched him pour her and him a drink while she paced the floor.

Ethan walked back with the drink in hand. "Do you plan on standing all evening? Or would you care to sit down?"

"If I'm going to the gallows, I'd prefer to stand," Kayla returned.

"Stop being so melodramatic." Ethan grabbed her by the arm and forced her down on the couch.

"Do you always manhandle women? Or do I alone have that special pleasure?"

Ethan took a deep breath. Kayla was testing his nerves. "Just you, my dear. I guess you bring out the caveman in me."

Kayla couldn't help but laugh at his comment.

"Finally." Ethan sighed. "You relax. You know this doesn't have to be unpleasant."

"Which part? The part where I disgrace my father by selling his company to his most hated enemy? Or sell myself for thirty pieces of silver?" Kayla took a huge gulp of her drink.

Ethan grimaced. "Well, when you put it like that it does." He turned to Kayla. "Listen, this is a win-win for the both of us. In exchange for marrying me, Adams Cosmetics will stay solvent and merge with Graham International. Everyone will keep their jobs and you will remain as president."

"And what do you get out of this arrangement?"

"I get to rectify one of my father's deepest regrets."

"So this is about Carter?" Kayla had been too young to remember Carter very well, but he had always been known as a heartless man.

"Partly." Ethan sipped his scotch. He didn't particularly want to discuss his relationship with Carter. "And I get you."

"This isn't about me. I'm just an added bonus. It's about making my father's company yours," Kayla finished. "Sounds like you get the better deal." She downed the rest of her vodka.

"I think you will enjoy it, as well."

"Is that so?" Kayla rolled her eyes upward at his arrogance. How could he be so sure of himself?

"Oh, I have no doubt you will enjoy the ways I intend to pleasure you," Ethan said in a low, raspy voice. He downed his scotch and put the decanter on the coffee table.

Kayla swallowed hard and her body trembled slightly. "I did not say I was accepting your offer." She scooted farther away on the couch from Ethan.

"Then why are you here?"

"I don't know." Kayla hung her head low.

"Oh, yes, you do," Ethan said, and before she knew it, he'd scooted next to her, pulled her drink out of her hands and set it down beside his. "You came here—" he reached out to grasp the back of her head "—because you've run out of options and you know you have no choice but to give in. So give in…" he said as he lowered his head and his lips descended on hers.

His mouth plundered hers like a pirate capturing a vessel.

When he lifted his head from the earth-shattering kiss, Kayla said, "I give in, okay? Are you happy now that you've won?"

"Not just yet," Ethan said, his eyes dark with desire. He leaned down and kissed her again. This time softly and gently. His tongue stroked hers with a hunger that was steadily rising. When she tried to protest, her lips parted and he took advantage of the ragged moan that escaped her. That's when Kayla knew she was fighting a losing battle.

Kayla felt Ethan's hands fumbling to pull her top up and cool air hit her skin. She didn't have any time to react, because Ethan had already pushed her satin bra aside and begun feasting on her breasts. It was the only way to describe the way he lavished each breast with gentle nibbles and wet flicks of his tongue. The touch of Ethan's hot tongue on her sent heat flooding through Kayla.

"Ethan…" she moaned.

Ethan grasped her hips and brought Kayla into direct contact with his arousal. She felt him rubbing against her and soon she was grinding against him, desperate to relieve the ache in her. Ethan knew he had to stop, otherwise he'd be taking her right there on the couch, and that's not how he intended to treat his future wife. Kayla wasn't like the other women he'd bedded. He actually cared about her, and if they had sex now she would think that's all there was between them. Sure, they'd have lustful moments as a couple and he couldn't wait to see her naked body, but he wanted their first time to be as husband and wife. Which meant they would have to get married quickly, otherwise he wouldn't be able to control himself.

Ethan pulled up on his haunches and looked down at Kayla. "I shouldn't have let things get that far…at least not yet."

Kayla pushed him away and sat up. Whenever she was with Ethan, he unleashed another side of her, one in which she had no control over her own body. She wasn't used to it, and she hated that he knew it. Kayla dragged her fingers through her hair, readjusted her bra and pulled down her top.

"Let's get some dinner," Ethan said, and offered Kayla his hand to stand up. "It's been an emotional day."

Kayla declined his hand and stood up on her own. "I guess I am a little famished, plus I need to figure out exactly what I'm going to tell my family. Because trust me, they will not be happy about this."

Instead of having his chef whip them up a meal, Ethan decided to grill up some steaks in the kitchen himself. He wasn't much of a cook, but he knew the basics. And he could use the time to show her his gentle side and move beyond the business talk that had dominated their relationship.

Kayla followed Ethan to the kitchen and was surprised when he pulled out rib-eye steaks and the ingredients for a salad from the refrigerator. She slid onto a stool at the island and watched him preheat the grill. "So you're going to make us dinner?"

Ethan looked up from the chopping board. "Does that surprise you?"

A smile spread across her face. "Actually it does. I didn't think the great Ethan Graham would subject himself to menial labor."

"I'm no chef," Ethan said as he shook seasoning across the steaks and chopped up iceberg lettuce to make a wedge salad. "But I make a mean steak on the grill."

Kayla's stomach growled and she blushed. "Sorry."

"How about a glass of wine?" Ethan said, grabbing a towel and wiping his hands.

"I would love some."

"I'll be back in a moment," Ethan said. Once he was gone, Kayla finally had a moment to think about the momentous decision she'd made. What was she doing? Her father would kill her when he found out. But what could she do? She had no other options.

Ethan returned with a bottle of Merlot and a corkscrew. "This is from the collection in my wine cellar. You'll love it," he said as he uncorked the bottle. He reached above her to grab two wineglasses that hung from the ceiling and poured them both a glass.

"To getting reacquainted." Ethan clicked his glass against hers. "So tell me all about Kayla." He looked intently at her.

Kayla sipped her wine. "What do you want to know?"

"Hmm…let me think." Ethan placed both steaks on the

grill before turning back around to answer her. "Well, are you a morning person or a night person?"

"Morning person. And you?"

"Night, of course. It's always more fun!" Ethan grinned devilishly.

"What's your favorite restaurant?" Kayla asked.

"Luiginos, it's a mom-and-pop place, but they make the best homemade gnocchi with vodka sauce that you've ever tasted. What's your favorite book?"

Kayla paused for a moment before answering. "*Little Women*. I love that Jo is so independent and passionate about being her own person, even back then."

Ethan laughed, turning over the steaks. "Of course, you would empathize with Jo. She's the eldest and is strong and independent, like a certain woman I know."

Kayla met his gaze evenly and sipped her wine. "And proud of it!"

Ethan smiled. For the first time, they were having a real conversation, one in which they weren't arguing or yelling at each other. And he had to admit, he loved it.

When the steaks were done, they sat down to enjoy them and the salad at the kitchen table. It was very informal, which surprised Kayla. She hadn't expected Ethan to be so laid-back. The conversation between them flowed easily from books to music to sports. She even found they were both Atlanta Hawks fans and shared a love of basketball.

"I have the best box seats," Ethan said. "We'll have to catch a game."

"I'm sure we'll have plenty of time once we're...uh...married." Kayla nearly choked out the word.

"Kayla." Ethan's dark eyes stared at her. "It's possible we can make this marriage work. We both just have to be willing to try."

"You make it sound so easy, Ethan." Kayla looked up at him and found it impossible to look away. Even now, he had a way of making her feel like a besotted teenager again. "But you and I both know that my family will never accept this. Ever."

Chapter 6

"Things are going to be fine." Ethan reached for Kayla's hand and squeezed it as they made their way to the front door of the Adams family mansion on Saturday evening.

"It's because of you that I'm in this mess," Kayla said, removing her hand from his grasp. She had spent the day at a hotel room, in part to hide from her family and their sad eyes and also because she'd needed time to get a hold of herself. After she'd left Ethan's last night, she'd been an emotional wreck. *Did he have any idea what he was doing to her? The effect he had on her?*

Ethan sighed. So they were back to sniping at each other even after their romantic dinner last night.

"It's because of me that your business will be saved," he said, trying to maintain an even tone.

"Don't remind me." She was making the ultimate sacrifice to protect her family legacy. Kayla used her key to open the front door. She stood in the hallway afraid to move. Ethan closed the door behind them.

"Well, you look beautiful," Ethan stated. The moment she'd come over to his estate that evening, he'd admired the sheath dress she was wearing. He loved the simplicity of the dress and how it clung to her curvy figure without revealing too much. Kayla would make the perfect wife.

"Thanks." Kayla looked back and forth down the hall.

"They do know we're coming, right?" Ethan nearly bumped into her when she tried to move out of view of the hallway.

Kayla shook her head. "No. I just told them I was calling a family meeting."

"So I'm walking into the lion's den?" Ethan commented.

Kayla turned around to face him. "Don't tell me you're scared?" She laughed tritely. "I didn't think the great Ethan Graham would be afraid of anyone."

Ethan paused. He wasn't looking forward to incurring Byron's wrath, but there was no avoiding it. Eventually he said, "I'm not afraid."

Kayla wasn't sure she believed him, but she didn't have time to hold his hand. She had to go into the family room and tell her father, her family, that she was marrying the enemy. What hurt the most was that she would be disappointing her father. But what choice did she have? She would do anything to save his life's work, even if it meant making a deal with the devil. "Let's go." Kayla stalked toward the family-room door.

"You're going to do what?" her father yelled, minutes later after she revealed she was engaged to Ethan. "Over my dead body!"

"Byron, please!" her mother cried, grabbing his arm.

"Elizabeth." He pointed to his beloved wife. "My daughter will not marry that man." Her father jumped off the couch and came walking toward Kayla with such fury in his eye that Ethan stepped in between them. "What the hell do you think you're doing, Graham? Do you honestly think I would harm my own child? That might be something your father might have done, but not me. Now move aside."

"Byron!" Her mother was horrified by her father's comment. "Was that really necessary?"

Both men were over six feet and within each other's eyesight, and Kayla hoped this wouldn't become a brawl. "Sir, I know you would never hurt Kayla, but I would be remiss if I did not protect my future bride."

"Your future bride?" Her father's eyes flashed with outrage. "Like hell!"

"Kayla, why are you doing this?" Shane finally spoke. He'd been stunned into silence at their sudden announcement and had to sit on the couch. "I thought you said you had no feelings for this man."

"I lied," Kayla said under Shane's steady scrutiny. The only way her family would accept this story is if she made it believable. "You all know I've had a crush on this irresistible man since I was a teenager." Kayla grabbed Ethan's arm for effect and stared up at him lovingly.

"But you're a grown woman now, and you'd made it clear that you'd outgrown your schoolgirl crush," Shane added.

"I was wrong," Kayla replied. "Ethan and I have been seeing each other since he returned to Atlanta."

"What did I miss?" Courtney asked as she rushed into the room. She'd been late to the foray as usual. Courtney grabbed a glass of champagne sitting on the coffee table.

"Ethan and Kayla are engaged," Shane answered.

Courtney spit out her champagne and had to wipe the

residue from her mouth with the back side of her hand. "Say what?"

"It's true." Kayla nodded in agreement.

"Listen, Mr. Adams, you know I respect you…" Ethan began.

"Then don't insult my intelligence that my daughter has suddenly fallen head over heels for you," Byron said, "and tell me the truth." He turned to Kayla. "What does he have on you?"

Tears blinded Kayla's eyes and choked her voice, forcing her to move away. "Daddy, please." She rushed over to a nearby ottoman. She was feeling weak in the knees at deceiving her family.

Ethan could see Kayla faltering so he came and wrapped his arm around her shoulders. "Kayla is with me of her own free will," he responded. "I knew Kayla had feelings for me as a teenager, but she was much too young for me to act on them." Then Ethan went in for the kill. "But that hasn't been the case now. Kayla and I have been sharing a bed for weeks." Ethan heard Kayla's sharp intake of breath at his audacity, but he continued, "Isn't that right, Courtney? You saw us making out at the Atlanta Steeplechase event."

All eyes turned to Courtney for confirmation. Courtney nodded. "It's true, Daddy. I caught Ethan and Kayla kissing in the stables weeks ago."

"And that day in your office?" Shane stared at Kayla. "I knew I had interrupted you two during the middle of something, but I never imagined…" His voice trailed off and he ran his fingers through his curly fro.

"All right. You're lovers," her father said. "I can accept that." He pushed past Ethan and kneeled down in front of Kayla who was sitting on the ottoman. "But you don't have to do this, Kayla. You don't have to marry the man. If you need to get over the schoolgirl fantasy you had over him, then do it, but baby girl, please don't tie yourself to this man for life."

"It's more than that, Daddy. We share a love of business, which is why—" Kayla stood up and faced her family "—I have signed an agreement which will allow Graham International to purchase the thirty-seven and a half shares, currently on the market, in addition to thirteen of my shares."

"Kayla, no!" Her mother shook her head in despair.

"That means, you'll have over 50 percent." Byron rose from his knees and glared at Ethan. "Making you majority shareholder and in control of Adams Cosmetics."

"That is correct, sir."

"So this was your scheme all along, wasn't it?" Byron asked. "Get my daughter to fall for you so she could turn over our family business to you."

"Daddy, you make me sound gullible and naive."

"Enough, girl!" Her father held up his hand. "I hope you're happy, Graham. You finally were able to get revenge for your father because I left GI and started my own cosmetics firm which is ten times better than anything GI has ever done. And now you got your grubby hands on my company. I hope you choke on it." Her father stormed out, leaving her mother crying in her handkerchief. Shane walked to the bar and poured himself a whiskey.

Only Courtney came up to congratulate them, or so Kayla thought. "Congratulations, sis!" She gave Kayla a hug and whispered, "I hope you know what you're doing, because you just broke our father's heart." And with that comment, she walked over to their mother on the couch and escorted her out.

"Shane." Kayla looked to her brother, but he just shook

his head and went out the side door to the terrace. Seconds later, she heard glass shattering on the concrete.

"Ohmigod, what have I done?" Kayla began crying uncontrollably.

"In time, they will understand," Ethan said, pulling her into his arms. "In time they will see that you did what you had to, to save this family." But Kayla was hearing none of it, she was just sobbing in his arms. A feeling deep in Ethan's gut took over him. He didn't recognize it at first, but then he realized he wanted to protect her, to shelter her from harm and ensure no one ever hurt her again.

When had that happened? Marrying Kayla was supposed to be about business, about creating a partnership between two successful people and merging her niche company with his conglomerate. Or so he'd told himself. When had he begun developing feelings for this woman? He didn't know when it had happened, but it had, and now he wanted to do right by her.

"I promise you, Kayla. I promise you I will make this right."

"Wow!" Piper was shocked. "You and Ethan engaged! I never saw that coming." When Kayla had asked to have a girls' lunch the next afternoon on the spur of the moment, Piper had definitely not expected to hear that news. "And you're getting married? Did I miss a step somewhere?"

Kayla shook her head. "No, you haven't."

"Then what? How did this all come about?"

"I was backed into a corner," Kayla replied honestly. Piper was the only person she could confide in. "That's how."

Piper threw her head back and laughed. "That doesn't sound like the Kayla I know. How did Ethan manage that feat?"

"This isn't funny, Piper."

"Okay, okay. Take it from the top."

"Well, you know I told you we shared a moment at the premiere where we almost kissed."

"Yes. I remember."

"Well, I went to Ethan's house to tell him that I wasn't interested and before I knew what was happening, we were kissing. That's when Ethan got it into his head that he wanted me."

"I don't see how that's necessarily a bad thing. It has been a while since someone's evoked that kind of passion in you."

"Thanks a lot, Piper." Kayla rolled her eyes, but she continued, "Anyway, he came to me with a proposition."

"Which was?" Piper reached for her drink and took a large gulp.

"Graham International would invest the money necessary in exchange for my marrying Ethan."

Piper nearly choked on her drink and coughed several times. Once she'd composed herself, she asked, "Ethan wants you for himself and in exchange he saves your family company? Admittedly, his method is over the top, but I admire a man who goes after what he wants, and clearly that's you."

"At what expense?" Kayla inquired. She brushed away a hot tear. "My whole family is against this marriage. And they weren't too happy to hear I sold Ethan their shares and mine to make him majority shareholder."

Piper nodded. "There is that."

"Piper, you know my family means the world to me. To go against their wishes—"

"You mean against your father's wishes."

"Same difference."

"No, it's not." Piper stared at her best friend. "You have

always been your father's daughter, so I know it's killing you to be at odds with him."

Kayla gulped hard and tears spilled down her cheeks. "You have no idea. This morning at breakfast, my father wouldn't even look at me. I couldn't bear it anymore, so I called you. I needed someone to help talk me through this. Everything is happening too fast. My head is spinning."

"Like your feelings for Ethan, bubbling to the surface?"

"What are you talking about?"

"Kayla, to be honest with you," Piper said, "I don't think you've ever gotten over the man. You've never really given any other man a real chance, because they didn't compare to Ethan."

"That's not true," Kayla replied, shaking her head furiously even though deep down she knew Piper was right. "What about Ayden?"

"As soon as things got serious and Ayden mentioned marriage, you used work as an excuse. And now that Ethan *has* shown genuine interest in you, you're scared to death."

"Am not." She didn't like that Piper could read her so accurately. She was scared. She was scared of the feelings that Ethan brought out in her. She didn't consider herself a wanton woman, but every time she was around him, she felt like she was on fire.

"Liar!" Piper called her out. "You do realize what marrying the man will entail."

"I do," Kayla responded, "which is why I have a proviso."

"Which is?"

"That our marriage is in name only."

"You mean no sex?" Piper asked, then threw her head back and laughed again. "Exactly who would that benefit? You would both be miserable and sexually frustrated."

"If we never consummate it, after some time has passed

I can have it annulled. Adams Cosmetics would be solvent by then."

"And you don't think Ethan Graham hasn't thought of every scenario? He doesn't strike me as the type not to have all his bases covered."

"Well, maybe he has never met his match before."

"Those are big words, Kay. I hope things work out how you hope."

"I can't believe the lengths you've gone to protect this family," Shane said from the doorway of her office midweek. He'd taken time to let the news of Kayla's engagement to Ethan settle, but it still stuck in his craw.

"What are you talking about?" Kayla looked up from the speech she was preparing that would announce the merger of Adams Cosmetics with Graham International.

Shane walked toward her. His misgivings were increasing by the minute. "I know what you're doing, sis. You don't have to put up a front with me. You might have to do it for Dad and Mom, but not me. I know you."

Kayla's eyes welled up with tears and her younger brother came over to embrace her, but she shook her head. "Shane, don't. You will ruin my makeup for the press conference."

"And we have plenty of makeup artists that can repair it for you. So let's sit for a minute." Shane grabbed her hand and forced her to sit with him on the couch. "So you sacrifice yourself to save this family by marrying Ethan? Kay, this is above and beyond the call of duty. We don't expect you to give up your life for us, for this company."

"I'm not." Kayla said the words but avoided looking in Shane's hazel eyes, afraid he would see the truth.

"You are merging Adams Cosmetics with Graham International, the corporate goliath you vowed we'd never be a part of, and on top of that you're marrying the man you claim you no longer have feelings for. And you say you're not giving up your life? I beg to differ."

Kayla hung her head low. "Wow! When you put it like that, it makes it seem like not only am I giving up my life but sacrificing my principles, too."

Shane shrugged. "If the shoe fits." When Kayla sniffed, he wrapped his muscular arms around her shoulders. "Listen, kid. I may not agree with your method, but no matter what, we're still family, and I will always be here to support you."

"Me, too." Courtney had suddenly appeared in her office. She stood stalwartly in her Dior suit, poised for battle. *Where had she come from? Had they decided to double-team her?*

Kayla and Shane both stood up and Courtney joined them in a group hug. "You have always got us," Courtney said, and Kayla immediately felt better. She didn't see Ethan step away from her doorway.

Ethan stood outside of Kayla's office, amazed at the family solidarity Kayla's siblings were presenting. Despite how they'd felt days ago, when she'd announced their engagement and the company merger, they still vowed to stand by her side. He doubted Carter Graham would have done the same for him. He would have disowned him. He guessed that's why he'd always wanted to be part of the Adams family. And now he would be.

Shane came walking out moments later and noticed Ethan standing there. "Ethan." He nodded.

"Shane, I'm glad to see you're here for Kayla. She was upset the other night when everyone walked out on her."

"Well, that's what families do, Ethan. We may argue and maybe even yell, but we stand together. So let me give you a piece of advice if you want to make it in this family." Shane came closer to face Ethan and whispered, "Don't ever try to come between Kayla and her family again. Otherwise, you'll find you'll remain an outsider and that's not a pleasant place to be. I'll see you at the conference." Shane gave him a salute.

Ethan watched Shane walk away. He had no intention of coming between Kayla and the Adamses again, but she was about to become his wife and possibly the mother of his children one day, so he would not be pushed aside like he didn't exist. He would make his presence known.

"Are you sure you're ready to do this?" Courtney asked from the other side of the wall. "Because if you want to make a run for it, I know a quick exit."

"There will be no running," Ethan said from the doorway with his arms folded across his chest. "Kayla knows what's at stake."

Courtney spun on her heel. "This was a private conversation between me and my sister."

"Then you should have closed the door," Ethan replied.

Courtney glared at him. She turned around and squeezed Kayla's shoulder. "Come downstairs to hair and makeup and I'll have Viola touch you up, okay?" She wiped a stray smudge off Kayla's face.

"Okay. Thanks." Courtney held up her fist and Kayla gave her a fist bump before she left her office.

"If looks could kill, I would be dead as a doorknob with the look your sister just gave me."

"Honestly, what did you expect, for them to be your biggest fan?" She gave him a brutal and unfriendly stare.

"Wow!" Ethan held up his hands at the hostility emanating off Kayla. Where was the pliable woman he had kissed and who had been putty in his hands? "A little less sarcasm, fiancée, would be nice."

"C'mon, Ethan." Kayla buttoned up her suit jacket and smoothed down her skirt. "We are not the average couple. Never will be. Which is why I'd like to suggest an addendum to your proposal." She walked to her office door and promptly shut it so they could have some privacy.

Ethan stepped back and leaned against Kayla's desk so he could watch her sashay back over to him. He loved the way her hips moved when she walked. "What did you have in mind?"

"I want a platonic marriage." Kayla cut right to the point. "In name only."

"Hell no!" Ethan roared, standing up straight.

"You haven't heard my argument," Kayla began, maintaining her composure at his outburst. "I am willing to turn my head to any dalliances you may wish to have."

"And you would expect me to do the same no doubt?" Ethan mocked.

"I suppose, yes." Though Kayla couldn't foresee any man making her feel quite the way Ethan did. It was why she didn't want to become intimate with him. If he had her off-kilter with a kiss and a few caresses, imagine what the full-court press would feel like? She might lose herself, lose her edge and then he would really have her where he wanted her—in and out of bed.

"You really don't want to share a bed with me?" Ethan asked, coming to her and circling his arms around her waist. "Is making love with me really such a repulsive thought?"

Kayla hated that her heart was beating fast at being in his arms again. "Let me go." She struggled to get out of his firm grasp, but Ethan wasn't budging.

Ethan leaned down until his head was inches from hers. "Not a chance, my dear. It will be my way or no way."

"Why are you doing this?" Kayla asked frantically. "You're getting what you wanted all along, and that's Adams Cosmetics. Why do I have to be part of the bargain?"

Ethan smiled devilishly. "You're an added bonus." Kayla went to slap him, but Ethan caught her hand and put it behind her back. "Oh, someone's feisty today."

"I hate you," Kayla said. Not only did he have a hold on her financially but physically.

"You may hate me now," Ethan said, "but when I have you moaning out my name in a few weeks you will feel differently." He swooped down to take her lips with expertise and began thoroughly exploring her mouth. He savored every honeyed crevice and dipped his tongue deeper for a taste of her sweet nectar. She was addictive.

Kayla hated that she succumbed to the domination of his lips. He had a tantalizingly persuasive method of getting her to acquiesce to him, and her traitoress body gave in every time. When he finally lifted his head, Kayla used the opportunity to move away. "All you've proven is that my body is not indifferent to you, Ethan. So you can have it, but you will never have my heart."

As they stood as a united front announcing their engagement and the merger to the rest of the world, Kayla's cold words stayed with Ethan.

Ethan didn't know why it bothered him so much that she would freely give her body to him, but her heart was off-limits. He'd never intended the union to be more than a marriage between two passionate individuals who shared a love of the same thing: big business. *So why did he feel like he had to win her heart, too? Because...ever since he'd first seen Kayla again, he'd felt strong feelings for her, feelings he'd thought he'd buried years ago, feelings he was having a hard time ignoring.*

"Everyone always thought you'd be the perennial bachelor, and this engagement is quite sudden, Mr. Graham," one reporter commented, cutting into his thoughts. "Is this a marriage of love or convenience?"

Kayla couldn't or didn't speak at that moment. It was obvious to everyone, including the press, that it was the latter, but Ethan refuted it.

"Sorry to disappoint you." Ethan came forward to the microphone. "But this marriage is one of love." He turned back and glanced at Kayla. "Kayla and I have known each other since we were kids. And there's always been something there, but we never acted on it until now."

"A source in the cosmetics industry says that Adams Cosmetics is crumbling financially. Does this have anything to do with the quick engagement?"

"Would your source happen to come from their competitor, Jax Cosmetics? If so, they would be misinformed." Ethan could feel Kayla tense at his side at the mere mention of the Jacksons. "I am more than happy to help my fiancée's family company and my board is in agreement that Adams Cosmetics is a good fit for Graham International. As you know, we already have a small cosmetics division, which Byron Adams used to be a part of."

"And you will be merging the two?"

"Absolutely," Ethan answered. "Kayla will be helming both divisions to ensure a smooth transition, but make no mistake, Adams Cosmetics is the main line." He glanced at Kayla, hoping that hearing the news would make her feel better, but her expression was blank. He had no intention of dismantling Adams Cosmetics. Instead, he intended to utilize her knowledge to help boost the other line.

"Thank you all for coming." Michael came to the microphone. "I'm sure you'll all be surprised with what Adams Cosmetics has in store for you in the future."

"I hope you're happy now," Kayla said as she walked forward and circled her arms around Ethan's waist. He watched Kayla put on a fake smile so the press could take a picture of them as a happy couple. He knew he had a long way to go if he ever intended to win her heart.

Chapter 7

"I don't know why Graham is putting on such a large wedding," her father commented poolside several weeks later at their estate, "when everyone at this table knows it's a farce."

The entire family was gathered for a pre-Memorial Day barbecue. He'd had the chef cook up some baby-back ribs, burgers, baked beans, potato salad and provide fresh lemonade. Since Kayla had announced her engagement, it had been a rare occasion that they were all together. It seemed as if everyone in the family was avoiding what was happening, but Kayla didn't have that luxury. Ethan was doing everything in his power to make their wedding the most elaborate, the most luxurious Atlanta had ever seen.

"Byron," her mother said from the table where she was reading a book. "It is Kayla's wedding and she deserves the very best. Don't you want that for her?"

Even though Kayla had tried her best to hide it, Elizabeth knew why her daughter was marrying Ethan—to save the company. But she was determined to make the best of a bad situation, even though her husband had made no such efforts.

Although Kayla was in the pool on a floating lounger, she was curious to hear the answer and turned to her father.

"Of course I do," he returned, putting down the burger he was about to munch on. "But not to Ethan Graham of all people."

Kayla sighed. "Daddy, what's done is done. There's no going back. The wedding planner has been hired, the invitations have been sent."

"Have you found a wedding dress yet?" Courtney asked.

"No." Kayla shook her head. Due to the rushed wedding day, it was impossible to have a custom gown made. Ethan had had several designer gowns flown in, but Kayla had put the kibosh to them.

"You do realize time is running out," Courtney replied as she sprayed on some sunblock. "There is only one week left to the wedding."

Kayla took a deep breath. "I recognize that, Courtney."

"Then chop chop." Once she was done, Courtney walked to the buffet and reached for the fruit salad bowl and added a healthy amount to her plate.

Kayla turned to Shane at her side. "No comment from you?" Shane had been silent for weeks now. He'd said he would support her, but he said very little recently.

"I thought my silence would be welcome," Shane returned. "Now if you'll excuse me. I'm heading to the lab." He'd just finished piling on the barbecue and filling his belly and now he needed to get back to work.

"Do you think you have the fragrance nailed now?" Kayla asked, getting out of the pool and wrapping one towel around her midriff and toweling her hair with another.

"I can't predict magic, Kayla," Shane responded. "But yes, I am close."

"Glad to hear it. I think we could use a boost around here." She walked over and kissed him on the cheek.

Shane quirked his brow questioningly. "What was that for?"

"Can't a girl kiss her brother?"

A smile ruffled Shane's mouth. "Of course, you can." He kissed her back. "I'll see you all later tonight." He waved before walking away.

"Is there anything I can do, dear, to help you with the wedding?" her mother inquired when Kayla joined her at the table to make herself a plate.

"There's tons." Kayla added a turkey burger, baked beans and potato salad to her plate. "The wedding planner wants to review the flower arrangements for the reception and discuss place cards."

"I'm at your disposal."

"I'm going to the country club," her father huffed and pushed away from the table. He didn't give her mother or Kayla a kiss before leaving, which didn't go unnoticed.

"Will he ever get over this?" Kayla asked, sitting down. She was afraid he was going to protest and refuse to walk her down the aisle. And if he did, Kayla didn't know if she could go through with the wedding without him.

"In time he will," her mother answered. "But your father is a proud man, and to see his life's work back at Graham International after leaving over twenty years ago is a rather hard pill to swallow. But give him time. He'll come around."

When Kayla looked doubtful, her mother smiled and added, "Or I will make him."

Kayla leaned over and gave her mother a hug across the table.

"Do we have to have all this sentiment?" Courtney asked. "Because it's a real drag."

"How's the wedding planning coming along?" Daniel asked Ethan later that evening over some beer. They were blowing off steam playing pool at the gentleman's club they often frequented.

"Surprisingly, very smoothly," Ethan answered. "With one exception."

"Which is?" Daniel asked, leaning over the pool table with his cue. "Red ball, right pocket." He knocked the ball into the hole.

"Kayla hasn't found a dress."

"The wedding is in a week!"

"I know that." Ethan swigged his beer. It couldn't come soon enough. He'd self-imposed celibacy until the wedding because he wanted his and Kayla's first time making love to be special, but his anatomy wasn't pleased with him. Whenever they were together, he had a hard time controlling his desire for her.

"Do you think she's using it as a stall tactic?" Daniel inquired. "Green ball, middle pocket." The ball missed the pocket and landed in the middle of the table, a clean shot for Ethan. Daniel was a king at pool, having played it in college, but threw Ethan one every now and again for his ego's sake.

Ethan shrugged. "Doesn't matter, because Kayla will marry me if she's wearing nothing but a smile. Green ball, left pocket." He slid the cue down and expertly shot the ball.

Daniel chuckled at Ethan's bluntness. "Your male guests wouldn't have a problem with it, though I suspect the ladies might be a tad embarrassed."

Ethan glared at Daniel. "Very funny." He wasn't smiling at all. He didn't want any other man looking at Kayla ever.

She was his, and in a week it would be official. "But I know what the problem is. Orange ball, corner pocket." He slid the cue behind him and shot the ball in the pocket.

"Show-off," Daniel said, laughing. "So you're a mind reader now?"

"When it comes to Kayla, yes I am," Ethan responded honestly. In the past few weeks, he'd come to read her quite well. He knew when to push and when to back off. "Kayla hasn't found a dress because it will make the wedding real to her."

"And she's just now realizing that?" Daniel asked. "You guys made the announcement. It's out in the open."

"I know that," Ethan said. "But Kayla is fighting her desire for me. She is desperate to maintain her independence and appear unaffected, but I intend to break through her defenses."

"Sounds like you're developing feelings for the woman as well," Daniel commented, looking at his boss.

"Who, me?" Ethan said in a somewhat high-pitched tone.

"Yeah, you." Daniel pointed his cue stick at Ethan. "Are you falling for Kayla? I mean you have gone out of your way to make this the wedding of her dreams, enlisting her best friend, Piper, to find out what Kayla dreamed about as a little girl."

"That was pretty slick of me, huh?" Ethan was proud of his scheme. At first Piper had been reluctant to meet with him, but once she heard the reason for his call, the redhead had been on board. Thanks to Piper, he'd ensured the wedding planner had every idea Kayla had ever dreamed of for her wedding day.

Kayla may think their marriage might be short-term, but Ethan had no such delusions. He wanted to get married once, just like his parents. Sure, his father had been a jerk, but he'd waited until he'd found Ethan's mother, Eleanor, before getting married. Ethan was the same. He'd always known there was something special about Kayla. He remembered one day when he'd come across a young Kayla and Piper riding their horses. Kayla was the cutest little thing with the biggest dimples he'd ever seen. When the horse had gotten spooked and thrown Kayla, Ethan had caught her before she hit the ground.

He knew she thought he was only marrying her to get his hands on Adams Cosmetics, but she was wrong. He may not love her in the same way Carter probably loved his mother, but he cared for Kayla deeply and wanted the best for her.

"Yeah, that was pretty slick of you, Ethan," Daniel said when Ethan missed his next shot because he'd lost focus. "Now all you have to do is get the lady over the broom."

"Oh, trust me, Kayla and I will be husband and wife."

"This is the one," Kayla said as she stood on a pedestal in one of the guest rooms and admired the gown in the three-section mirror the wedding planner had brought over for the occasion. Despite it being a holiday, she'd come so Kayla could finally get this dress business sorted out.

"It's stunning, Kay," Piper gushed.

"You will be a beautiful bride." Her mother wiped a stray tear with her handkerchief. It was the first time Kayla had let her sit in on one of the fittings. Kayla guessed her mother brought her good luck, because after a month, she had finally found the dress.

"Can you help me out of this dress?" Kayla said from the pedestal.

"Of course," Piper responded.

"I will let you get dressed, darling." Her mother kissed

her cheek. "I am so happy you found a gown. Now you'll see. Everything will be just fine." She patted Kayla's cheek.

"Thank you, Mama." Kayla gave her a tentative smile. Although she appreciated her words of encouragement, as the days drew near to her wedding day on the first of June, Kayla was a ball of nerves. When the big day came would she able to walk down the aisle and say "I do" to Ethan and commit to him for the rest of her life?

Kayla asked herself that same question on her wedding day that Saturday as she stared at her reflection in the mirror. She didn't even recognize herself. She was a June bride.

Viola, one of Adams Cosmetics' hairstylists and makeup artists, had come to the Adams estate to get her ready for the big day. And that she had. Kayla had opted for a half up, half down style with a tiara.

And the dress...well, she'd chosen a pearl color, which complemented her skin versus the traditional stark white. The soft shimmer satin was eye-catching and the bodice featured a figure-flattering asymmetrical waist with a captivating jeweled band. Bubble hems hung generously down the full bustled skirt. Kayla would certainly make an entrance in the designer gown.

"You look stunning," Courtney said as she added a few dabs of perfume to Kayla's wrists and ears.

Kayla glanced behind her. "Thank you, sis."

Courtney noted her less than enthusiastic response but didn't say anything.

"You okay?" Piper asked, leaning against Kayla's shoulder as she looked at her best friend in the mirror. She was maid of honor and was wearing a one-of-a-kind strapless satin emerald dress with a simple A-line skirt that complemented her vibrant red hair. Kayla had wanted to keep it simple yet elegant so that all eyes would be on her when she walked down the aisle.

"Of course." Kayla smiled.

Piper noticed that the smile didn't quite reach her eyes. "Courtney, can you give us a minute?"

"Sure. I'll go check and see how everything is going downstairs."

Once the door closed, Piper, turned back to Kayla. "Girl, if you have any doubts, now is the time to speak up."

"I've made my bed, Piper and now I have lie in it. Literally," Kayla added.

In the last month, Ethan had shown surprising restraint. The kisses they'd shared since were hungry and passionate, yet he hadn't tried to coerce her into his bed. She'd thought he'd be eager to claim his prize, but instead he seemed intent on waiting. Why wait? What was Ethan up to?

"We'll become lovers soon, and I just wonder how much I can trust him," Kayla said. "Look at how we got here."

Piper was about to respond when there was a knock on the bedroom door. "Are you decent?" A male voice inquired.

Kayla beamed when she heard her father's strong baritone voice on the other side. "Yes, we are, Daddy."

Her father walked in wearing a designer tuxedo and matching pearl-colored tie. He walked toward Kayla with his arms outstretched. "Baby girl, you look beautiful." He pulled her toward him and embraced her tightly. He leaned back to take another look at her and kissed her forehead.

"I'm going to give you guys some alone time," Piper said quietly before leaving.

"You know how proud I have always been of you, right?" her father asked once Piper had gone.

Kayla gave a halfhearted smile. "Yes, but it's always nice to hear."

"Then, I have to try once last time to convince you to stop this travesty," her father returned. "You don't have to do this, Kayla. You don't have to marry him."

"Daddy, what choice do I have, do we have?" Kayla looked deep into her father's eyes. They had an unspoken language between them, always had.

Resigned, her father looked down. He didn't seem to have an answer to the question that had been looming over all their heads for weeks.

"I guess we don't have a choice," her father replied grudgingly. "But know this, even though I'm giving you away to Graham, of all people, you will always be my sweetheart."

Tears bordered Kayla's eyes and she fanned her face. "Daddy, you can't make me cry now. It will ruin my makeup."

"I do have something to say and promise me you'll hear me out before you speak."

Kayla crossed her heart.

"This is a big day for you. And I want you to know that I recognize everything you have done for this family." Kayla began to speak, but her father silenced her with his index finger. "See…I knew you wouldn't let me finish. Listen, you don't have to admit it to me, but I know that you've tethered yourself to Graham in this unholy union to save Adams Cosmetics. And all I want to say is thank you."

Kayla wanted to correct him but opted to say only, "You're welcome."

If someone were to ask Kayla what she remembered about her wedding, she would say, "Not much." It was like she was walking in a dream. She would remember her father grasping her elbow and leading her down the aisle. She would re-member the tears of joy in her mother's eyes as she saw her in her wedding gown. She would remember Shane's stoic expression from across the aisle when her father joined her hand with Ethan's. Or the thumbs-up signal Piper gave her when she handed her the wedding bouquet so they could recite their vows.

And now Ethan had his hand on her waist, leading her around the reception so they could thank their guests for coming, making it seem even more surreal. Was she really Mrs. Ethan Graham? Had she really just married her father's worst enemy and her childhood crush?

"I can't wait to have you all to myself," Ethan whispered in her ear once when he thought no one could hear.

It caused Kayla's stomach to bunch up in knots. So much so that when it was time for dinner, she could hardly eat a bite. She just moved the food from one side of the plate to another.

"Are you feeling okay?" Ethan asked, whispering in her ear.

Kayla merely nodded. She tried to eat, but everything tasted like rubber. How on earth was she going to get through the day knowing she would become Ethan's lover later that night?

Ethan, on the other hand, was extremely happy with the day's events. He and Kayla were now legally joined in marriage. What was hers was his and what was his was hers. Sure, he'd thought about a prenuptial agreement, his lawyer had even insisted on it, but Kayla Adams was a woman of her word. She wouldn't try for a divorce, otherwise she would risk losing control of Adams Cosmetics, and that would never do. He would have to content himself with the fact that Kayla desired him. She may not love him, but that could change in time.

Ethan had watched as Kayla said her vows. She'd gone through the motions and said the required words, but there was no emotion behind them. And when he'd kissed her, she'd been as mechanical as a robot, but Ethan intended to change all that tonight. He would coax a passionate response from her and she would respond to him as the vibrant, sexy woman he knew her to be.

Kayla was returning from a trek to the restroom when she heard Shane and Courtney mention Ethan's name. She stayed behind some planters to listen to their conversation.

"Did you hear how Ethan recited his vows?" Shane asked Courtney.

"If I didn't know any better, I would have thought he meant them."

"I thought it was just me," Shane returned. "But the way Ethan looked at Kayla so intently when he said his vows made me almost believe him."

"I heard it, too." Courtney nodded. "Do you think Ethan is even capable of genuine emotion?"

"I don't know, sis," Shane said. "I just hope Kayla knows what she got herself into."

"If anyone does, it's Kayla. She's a big girl and quite capable of taking care of herself. Perhaps it's the other way around, and Ethan doesn't know what he got himself into."

Shane chuckled. Kayla was a force to be reckoned with. "Of course you're right, Courtney."

As Kayla watched them walk away, she wondered if they were right. Did Ethan really care for her? Or was he just good at putting on a performance in front of the crowd of family, friends and coworkers that had gathered for Atlanta's wedding of the year?

"Kayla, there you are," her mother cried from behind her. "Where have you been hiding?"

"I haven't been hiding." Kayla laughed nervously. *At least not really.* She'd been avoiding. She knew time was winding down before she and Ethan would have to leave for their honeymoon. She wasn't sure what Ethan had planned, but Kayla was anxious about what would come later.

"Ethan was looking for you," her mother said, "but he's with your father now."

"Oh, Lord!" Kayla glanced over her shoulder and saw that Ethan and her father were speaking. She had no idea what they were saying, but it couldn't be good. Byron Adams despised anything Graham. He had for years. Kayla had to go over and interrupt them before something bad happened.

"I don't know how you convinced my daughter to marry you, Ethan," Byron Adams said at his side, "but you had sure better take care of my baby girl. Otherwise you'll have me to answer to."

"I'm very well aware of your disdain for me, Byron," Ethan responded. "But make no mistake, I will take care of my wife and I promise no harm will ever come to Kayla."

Kayla came walking toward the duo just as she heard her father say, "I guess your word will have to be enough."

Kayla looked back and forth between the two men, but their faces were guarded. "Daddy, is everything okay?" She instantly walked to her father.

Ethan swallowed hard as he watched them embrace and Byron kiss her forehead. Kayla hadn't come to him first, she'd gone to Byron. The bond she shared with her father was a strong one and he didn't intend to come between them, but she would have to make room for Ethan in her life now.

"Kayla." Ethan lightly pulled her toward him. "Darling," he added for good measure and inserted her arm through his. "I think it's time we made our exit."

Kayla glanced at her father and then up at Ethan. "Oh, of course." She extracted her other arm from her father. Going forward she was no longer her father's daughter, she was Ethan's wife.

Soon, she was kissing her father, mother, Shane, Courtney and Piper underneath a cloud of rice as she and Ethan made their way to the limousine that waited for them outside. She blew them a kiss as she ducked inside.

Once they were on their way to the airstrip to board Ethan's private plane, Ethan removed his tie and loosened the button on his tuxedo shirt. "God, I'm glad that's over. Aren't you?" He looked over and saw Kayla sitting as far away from him as humanly possible and wistfully looking out of the window. "We are coming back, you know."

Kayla's head whipped around. "I know that." She turned back around to face the window.

Ethan scooted over until their thighs nearly touched. Kayla hated that he was so close to her because she knew whenever he turned up the seduction dial she was powerless. "Kayla, it's you and me from this point forward." His index finger tucked under her chin as he turned her face to him. "It doesn't have to be this way. Can't we find some common ground?"

"To peacefully coexist?" Kayla laughed. "You sure do want a lot from the woman you forced into marrying you. I'm here, aren't I? What more do you want?"

"I want this." Ethan lowered his head and took her lips.

His hands slid down the bodice of her wedding dress and brought her closer to him.

When he finally lifted his head, Kayla's eyes were closed and he could feel the rapid beat of her pulse. "And apparently you want this, too."

Kayla didn't have a fast retort, because truth be told, he was right. She'd been trying to fight it, but she wanted Ethan.

Chapter 8

The flight to their secret honeymoon destination did little to help Kayla's anxiety. To be on a plane with Ethan's sheer male magnetism for hours on end was playing havoc with her system. Sure, he'd pulled away from their stirring kiss during the ride to the airport because he knew what was to come. Once onboard, she'd politely declined his invitation to help her change. Kayla was sure Ethan would like nothing better than to help her out of her wedding dress, so she'd asked for assistance from the stewardess.

And now as they were landing, Kayla still had no idea where they were. All she knew was that it was someplace tropical, as she'd seen nothing but ocean for hours.

As she exited the plane, Ethan stood at the bottom of the staircase to help her down. "Welcome to Bora Bora, Tahiti, Mrs. Graham."

Kayla looked around her. "Tahiti." It was certainly a romantic destination for a honeymoon. "Nice touch." She gave a hesitant smile.

Ethan smiled back, "Glad you approve," he said as helped her into a limousine waiting on the tarmac before joining her inside. "You'll love where we're staying," he continued. "I spared no expense."

"I'm sure nothing but the best for Ethan Graham," Kayla said despondently, looking out of the window.

Ethan had not been lying. Kayla was floored by the stunning lagoon view from the two-story hillside villa of one of Bora Bora's finest resorts. There was a private waterfront balcony and she could see a vast array of brightly colored fish swimming in the water. The décor was Polynesian-style and complemented with rich mahogany wood flooring and furnishings.

Then of course there was the looming king-size canopy bed that reminded her of what was to come later that evening. The bathroom was done in Italian marble and had a separate shower and soaking Jacuzzi. The kitchen downstairs was stocked with everything they could possibly need from fruits, cheese, bread and meats, to paté, caviar and the finest champagne.

"Is everything to your liking, Mr. Graham?" the concierge asked Ethan.

"Everything looks good," Ethan said, walking him out. "I'm sure my wife and I will enjoy our stay."

"The refrigerator is well stocked," the concierge stated. "But should you want to come up for air—" he smiled knowingly "—there are excellent restaurants, pools, spas and leisure water activities at your fingertips, and that other item you requested is also well stocked."

"Thank you." Ethan had asked the concierge to ensure

there were half a dozen boxes of condoms waiting in the bedroom nightstand drawer. There would be plenty of time for babies later. Right now, he wanted Kayla all to himself.

Once the door had closed, Ethan walked back inside but found the room empty. He followed the sound of the water and saw Kayla standing outside facing the ocean. "So, Mrs. Graham, what would you like to do now?" His eyes danced with mischief.

"I don't know, Ethan. What did you have in mind?" Kayla asked, turning around to face him.

Ethan grasped Kayla around the waist and pulled her closer to him. "A lot of things come to mind," he returned. "But I'd rather think you might like a shower and maybe a nap to unwind before dinner."

Ethan saw the surprise register on Kayla's face. "Did you think I was going to throw you on the bed and have my way with you?" he inquired. When Kayla didn't answer, he responded, "I won't need to twist your arm." He lightly caressed her cheek and felt Kayla tremble underneath his touch. "We already want each other, so tonight we will finally do what comes naturally."

Kayla wiggled free from Ethan's grasp. "I…I'm going to get freshened up." She made a quick exit, leaving Ethan alone on the deck.

Ethan watched her go. Now that they were free from all distractions, he intended to make Kayla his in every way. Tonight, he would explore every inch of her body until she was crying out his name as he took her to new heights. Oh, yes, tonight was going to be immensely pleasurable.

Kayla glanced at her reflection in the mirror as she dressed for dinner. She'd thought Ethan would want to have

dinner in, so she'd been surprised when he'd suggested they
go to the resort's fine-dining restaurant.

She wore a simple print dress with a halter neck that
flowed to her ankles. Strappy sandals adorned her feet, accompanied by colorful shell jewelry on her earlobes and
neck, though one piece stuck out prominently: the huge
seven-carat diamond ring that Ethan had put on her left hand
that day.

"You look beautiful," Ethan said when Kayla came out
of the bathroom and found him waiting in the sitting area.

"Thank you," Kayla returned. "You, as well." It was all
she could muster, but what she was really thinking was that
he looked good enough to eat in his linen suit with matching shirt and tie.

Ethan held out his arm. "Let's go have some fun."

If anyone would have told Kayla that she would be enjoying her honeymoon night, she would have called them a liar,
but she was. The dinner was an eclectic fusion of Polynesian,
Pacific and Mediterranean influence, the wine was flowing
and the live band was spectacular. Kayla could feel herself
loosening up. So when Ethan asked her to dance, she didn't
turn him down.

Instead, she allowed him to wrap his arms around her and
sway her to the beat of the music. He dipped her, and when
he pulled back up, Ethan was looking at her intently, pas-
sionately. Before Kayla could gather herself, his lips were
sweeping across hers and she was responding to him.

Kayla told herself it was the wine or the moonlight, but
none of it was true. The moment his lips were on hers, Kayla's body took on a mind of its own and she forgot where she
was. Her arms circled around his neck, bringing her closer
to him. Her nipples puckered and strained against the fabric
in her dress, eager to be closer to Ethan.

Ethan pulled away first. "Not here," he whispered.

He quickly ushered her out of the restaurant and into a ca[r] that just so happened to be waiting for them. They reache[d] for each other the moment the doors were closed. Etha[n] pulled Kayla into his lap. Both his hands grasped the sides o[f] her face and then he kissed her so thoroughly and so deepl[y] that Kayla nearly lost consciousness. His hands palmed he[r] backside, pulling her flush against him.

Kayla didn't remember the car stopping or how they go[t] into their villa. She just remembered the lights being lo[w] enough to illuminate the villa with a light haze and pullin[g] Ethan by his tie onto the canopy bed in the bedroom. Sh[e] could hide it no longer; she wanted this man, she had fo[r] years and it was time she found out exactly what it was lik[e] to be made love to by Ethan Graham. She whipped off hi[s] suit jacket and flung it across the room.

"Slow down," Ethan said, grasping Kayla's hand in his[.] "We have all night. Hell, all week. I don't want to rush ou[r] first time together."

"Ethan, you don't have to try so hard to romance me,["] Kayla said. "You won, okay? I'm here. I want you, so let'[s] do this." She reached for his pants, but Ethan stopped her.

"Kayla, it wasn't all about winning for me," Ethan re[s]ponded. "I do care for you."

"Yes, I know. You want me. And I want you." She ros[e] from the bed to her feet. "There, I said it. What more do yo[u] want?"

"I want you to believe me," Ethan returned, "before w[e] take this any further."

"Are you serious?" Kayla asked, but when she turned an[d] looked Ethan in the eye, she could see he was very seriou[s] and it stopped her cold.

"I have always cared for you, Kayla," Ethan returned[.]

"Even when perhaps I shouldn't have, but I do. And you need to know that this is more than winning for me. Please tell me you believe that much about me."

"Why are you doing this, Ethan?" Kayla rushed toward the patio doors. "Isn't it enough that you have me? Why are you messing with my head?"

Ethan rushed after Kayla and caught her at the door. He hugged Kayla tight, but she resisted him, struggling in his arms, but he refused to let go. "I need you to believe me, Kayla." He kissed her forehead first and then her cheek and then her lips. He kept kissing Kayla until she stopped resisting him. "Say you believe me."

Kayla felt the knot of her halter dress come undone and Ethan lower his head to kiss her neck. He teased the tender spot on her nape with tender flicks of his tongue.

"I believe you," Kayla heard herself murmur in between moans as Ethan lifted her off her feet and brought her back to the bedroom. He laid her gingerly on the bed and began undressing her.

Kayla watched him remove his tie and slowly unbutton his shirt. Her breath caught in her throat when he removed his shirt and she could see his muscular arms, broad chest and hard stomach. And when he removed his pants to reveal muscular thighs and legs, Kayla thought she might die from desire. When he was down to his briefs, Ethan reached over the bed and slid the print dress down Kayla's body and flung it across the room. It landed near his discarded suit jacket.

Ethan smiled when he found Kayla wasn't wearing anything underneath except lace panties. He knew he'd felt her nipples earlier when they'd been dancing. Thankfully, he hadn't pinched them like he'd wanted to, otherwise they would have made a spectacle of themselves on the dance floor.

"You are so beautiful," Ethan whispered, joining Kayla on the bed and stroking her thigh. He slid her panties down her legs until she was completely naked.

Now he could do what he'd wanted to do for months, and that was feast on her. He started with her lips. They were so plump and alluring that he just had to possess them. He kissed her slowly and with masterful care, sipping at her lower lip before moving to her upper lip until she parted them both for his exploration. Her arms snaked around his neck and she nestled into his embrace. He took this as an invitation to thrust his tongue deeper into her mouth, and she sucked on it fervently.

Ethan groaned. Kayla was already starting to move underneath him. He knew he had to slow the pace and moved his lips from hers. He heard her slight protests, but only for a second because he was trailing hot, wet kisses down her neck to the valley between her breasts. When he came to one delicious round breast, his mouth latched onto one nipple and he licked and loved the sensitive tip with his tongue all the while kneading the other soft breast with his other hand. When he was done with one breast, he swapped and went to the other.

"Yes, Ethan," Kayla moaned. "Don't stop." Little bursts of pleasure detonated inside Kayla at each flick of his tongue. He was wicked with his tongue and knew how to exact a response from her. His hot hands burned her flesh as they lightly slid down her sides, skimming her waist, then her thighs. It felt so good and so right. Each touch was intoxicating, leaving her defenseless.

And it wasn't just his tongue; his hands made their way to the brown curls at the V of her thighs. He cupped her, petting her lightly, and her feminine lips opened like a flower to his searching fingers. His thumb was stroking that eager feminine pearl at the apex of her thighs. He worried the pearl with his thumb and she writhed in his arms, wanting to ease the ache between her legs.

"That's right, baby," Ethan cooed. "Enjoy it." He loved listening to the sounds of her passionate breathing. Kayla was becoming more and more wet as he slid his finger inside her. She shuddered at first, but her muscles soon embraced the delicious contact. As his fingers delved deeper, Kayla began to soar. He could feel her body begin to tremble, so he increased the rhythm of his fingers and bent his head to suckle harder on her breasts. That's when Kayla began to shudder uncontrollably and she cried out.

"Ethan—" She tried to catch her breath, but she couldn't. She was barely over her first orgasm when he slid down the bed and grabbed her hips, pulling her toward his mouth until he was facing her sex. He hooked her legs over his shoulders and then began to lap her. Kayla felt the flicker of his tongue on her and nearly became unglued as she was already sensitive down there. "Let…let me catch my breath."

"Soon, baby, soon," he said. Ethan was glad that Kayla had come, but he wanted more. His tongue slid inside the silk walls of her vagina and Kayla jerked. He savored her as if she were a cherry on top of a brownie sundae. He slid in and out of her sweet honey, clockwise and then counterclockwise with slow and controlled movements and then faster. He varied his sucks, licks and flicks until he was wet with her juices. She was sweet, heady and intoxicating, causing Ethan's tongue to sink deeper.

Kayla was experiencing a whirlwind of pressure building inside her until an explosion reached her core and she screamed. Her back arched, surrendering to the abyss of pleasure that overtook her, and her toes curled on his shoulder.

She was completely satiated and fell back onto the bed. "Has anyone ever told you that you are gifted?"

"Hmm, I'm glad you like," Ethan said, releasing her legs and sliding back up to the pillows.

"Oh, I more than liked it." Kayla smiled.

Once Kayla's breathing returned to some semblance of normalcy, she knew that she had achieved a climax and was languid, but Ethan needs had not been satisfied. So she leaned over to rain kisses over his broad chest, licking his nipples until they turned into hard ridges. She could hear his groans as she moved down to his flat stomach and trim waist until finally coming to the stiff ridge of his penis in his briefs.

She reached down and slid them down his legs. Never in her wildest girlish fantasies had she imagined Ethan would be so spectacular. His obvious arousal only inflamed Kayla further and she stroked him, slowly at first. He was sleek, taut and scorching hot, but it didn't deter her. She felt empowered that she could give Ethan the same pleasure he'd given her. She licked the full length of him, giving him slow, gentle and fast squeezes along the way. He filled her hand completely and did the same when she put him in her mouth. She lightly licked the head at the base before pulling him deeper in her mouth.

Ethan was in a sexual haze and could only lie there helpless as he succumbed to Kayla's ministrations on his throbbing member. He sank his hand into her curly hair, urging her to continue. He watched her pull up to look at him for a moment and smile as she flicked her tongue back and forth, squeezing his girth. His breath began to come hot and quick.

Kayla could feel Ethan teetering on the edge, so it didn't surprise her when he turned the tables and had her on her backside. She watched him reach inside the nightstand drawer and procure a condom. He protected them both and lifted her knees, then pressed the tip of his arousal against her opening, nudging inside. Her body slowly obliged and when he was sure she could take all of him, he thrust fully inside. Every hard, hot, powerful inch of him, and Kayla nearly came apart. To finally have him inside of her, the man she'd wanted her entire life. It seemed unreal, but it was happening.

"I have always wanted this," she murmured.

"So have I," Ethan groaned. His mouth covered hers hungrily, thrusting deep with his tongue while her body drew him in, allowing Ethan to glide in and out with a steady rhythm. He worked deeper inside her with each thrust until Kayla wasn't sure where he ended and she began. He covered her body with kisses, increasing the tempo until Kayla cried out in bliss. Ethan's hands curled around a knot of her hair and Kayla could her him chanting her name. Seconds later, he was growling against her ear and collapsed on top of her. He quickly rolled onto his side, relieving her of his weight.

"Wow! That was pretty incredible," Ethan said. He'd never expected the sex to be so intense with Kayla. He supposed it was because he finally cared about a woman he'd slept with. On some unconscious level he'd always known they would be great together. Perhaps that's why he'd fought it for so long. But now Kayla was his forever.

"It was," Kayla said, looking up at the ceiling fan. She'd always wanted to know how it would feel to be with Ethan. It had been the most meaningful lovemaking she'd ever had.

Kayla jerked awake. She blinked several times as the morning rays came through the wooden shutters of the villa.

She turned and found Ethan sleeping soundly on his stomach. It was hard to believe all that they'd shared the night before.

"I can keep doing this forever," Ethan had told her last night, his eyes glassy with desire.

"I don't want to stop, either," Kayla had assured him, and so they'd made love again and again. They'd made love until they couldn't get enough of each other and each experience was better than the last. Ethan had been an eager lover, and looking at the clock on the nightstand, she saw she'd barely gotten four hours of sleep. As she slipped naked out of bed, Kayla felt more like she was in a dream than reality. She was really Mrs. Ethan Graham.

Kayla grabbed Ethan's dress shirt lying on the floor and slipped her arms inside before walking out to the patio. The sky was cloudless and the ocean was a vibrant blue. Kayla stared out at the water.

When she'd been a young girl, she'd dreamed of being in Ethan's arms, and last night had not disappointed. She loved the taste, the touch and the feel of him. It had assaulted all of her senses and in turn it had opened her very soul to him. Of course, Ethan had no idea of her true feelings. And he never would. Kayla would let him continue to think that theirs was a natural chemistry that had been underlying between them for years. There was no way Kayla would tell Ethan she loved him and give him that kind of power over her. He already had her company hanging over her head, so she refused to give him the added satisfaction.

Kayla didn't hear a creak on the patio floorboard, she just felt Ethan's hot breath on her neck seconds before his lips kissed the back of her neck. He nibbled on her neck and suckled. He sucked until Kayla's head leaned back on his shoulder and she began to melt against his hard chest and rock-hard penis. *Was he naked outside?* Ethan began massaging her breasts through his shirt and Kayla couldn't help but moan aloud.

"Let's take this back inside," Ethan murmured as lust surged through him. He could feel his penis getting harder.

Kayla turned around to face him and fused her lips with his. Ethan grabbed her buttocks, lifting her off the floor so Kayla could wrap her legs around him. Slowly, he walked backward into the villa, all the while keeping their mouths joined.

They fell back together on the bed, a mass of naked limbs. His lips came down on hers and warmth rushed through her. His mouth commanded hers as his fingers threaded through her hair. Kayla was breathless, which gave Ethan enough time to throw her off guard. He bent down and lifted the shirt to her waist and went right to the apex at her thighs.

He kissed, nibbled and licked the sweet nub until he found the precise flicker that set her aflutter. Her body told him when he reached the sweet spot because Kayla arched off the bed and raw-edged whimpers escaped her lips.

Ethan continued his quest by kissing his way up her leg and tracing the smooth contours of her thighs. Kayla assisted him by removing his shirt, giving Ethan easy access to feast on her bare breasts. He rolled atop her and used his thighs to spread her legs and entered in one swift thrust. They moved together, skin-to-skin, riding wildly. When Kayla lifted her hips, Ethan seemed to understand her pleas and pulled in and out with delicious ecstasy. An undeniable hunger seemed to fuel them and they both galloped quickly to an orgasm.

"Ohmigod!" Kayla came first, crying out with delight, and her inner muscles clamped around his throbbing member, holding him captive until he collapsed on top of her.

Chapter 9

Hours later, Ethan and Kayla were still in bed.

"Is it your intention to keep me on my back our entire honeymoon?" Kayla inquired, pushing several pillows up so she could lean back.

Ethan rested his face on his hand, looked up at Kayla and smiled broadly. "I had thought about it."

"Hmm...I'm not saying I mind," Kayla responded, "but I am a little hungry."

"I guess I have been remiss in my husbandly duties by not feeding you." Ethan leaned over to grab the phone. "I'm not really in the mood to cook, so how about I have something delivered?"

"Sounds fabulous."

Kayla and Ethan gorged on Polynesian chicken, mango beef, coconut rice, baked sweet potatoes and guava cake while lying in bed. They hadn't moved much out of the bedroom the entire day, other than to enjoy a tantalizingly long, hot shower together.

"This is delicious," Kayla said, sipping on the watermelon mai tai that had accompanied the meal.

"I couldn't agree more. Cheers!" Ethan clicked his glass against Kayla's. "So is there anything that you would like to do while we're here?"

"You mean besides seeing you naked?" She smirked, pulling down the sheet so she could feast her eyes on his incredible pectorals.

"Yeah, besides sex."

"I would love to go snorkeling," Kayla commented.

"I love your adventurous spirit," Ethan stated. He leaned across the bed and grabbed her hand. "You're on."

Kayla and Ethan's week in Bora Bora was filled with making love, eating, sunbathing and a little bit of sightseeing thrown in for good measure. On their third day on the island, they finally emerged from their villa to take a tour with one of the local vendors to Bora Bora Lagoonarium and do a little snorkeling.

"You look hot." Ethan gave a catcall whistle when Kayla emerged from the bedroom wearing a leopard-print string bikini.

"You like?" Kayla spun around on her flip-flops.

"Hmm, I more than like." Ethan reached for her, but Kayla pushed his hands away.

"Don't start," Kayla said, wrapping her cover-up around her waist. "Otherwise we'll end up back in bed, and I'm not complaining, as I've enjoyed every moment, but we've haven't been out of this villa in two days."

Ethan smiled broadly. "That's because I can't get enough of my beautiful, sexy wife."

"C'mon." Kayla grabbed her straw bag, large-brim hat

to keep the sun out of her face and sunglasses and headed toward the door.

They joined another couple of honeymooners at the main building of the resort to take a yacht over to the Bora Bora Lagoonarium.

"It's really beautiful out here," Kayla said once they were on deck and zipping through the ocean on a yacht.

"And serene." Ethan slid behind Kayla and wrapped his arms around her middle and rested his chin on her shoulder. "Makes you want to stay out here forever."

"Of course that won't be the case for too much longer," Kayla commented, staring out over the ocean. They would have to go home eventually, and she knew it would be business as usual for Ethan. She'd caught a glimpse of the man under the ruthless corporate raider she'd always known, when he'd shared what it was like growing up with Carter as a father and constantly trying to live up to his expectations. His mother had been his escape and the person he turned to until she'd passed away.

Ethan frowned. It was the first mention Kayla had made of returning to the States. He wondered if things would change between them once they were back home. He'd broken through Kayla's hard exterior shell and they were enjoying themselves, but Ethan was sure he had not even touched the surface of how she felt emotionally toward him. Kayla had a wall up the size of Mount Everest. He doubted he could break through her defenses in a week, but he'd certainly try.

The yacht suddenly stopped and the tour guide said, "All right folks, grab a mask and snorkel and jump right in."

And that's exactly what they did. Kayla took a mask and snorkel from the large bin and jumped into the famous turquoise-blue water. Ethan was soon behind her and they were swimming into the lagoon.

The water was warm against Kayla's skin and the ocean clear. Kayla could easily see all the different fishes in the lagoon, from turtles to sharks to stingrays.

When Ethan came to swim beside her, Kayla pointed to a nearby stingray. Ethan grasped her hand under the water and led her to another area that held a wide array of fish species.

They stayed in the lagoon for nearly two hours. When they returned to the boat, Polynesian music and rum runners awaited them. Ethan grabbed two and handed one to Kayla.

"Cheers!" Ethan lifted his glass.

"Cheers!" Kayla smiled back at him.

On their fourth day in Bora Bora, Ethan arranged for a tour of the island by 4x4 Range Rover. They drove along the rugged coastline and got to see Bora Bora's tropical floral life that lined the hills and valleys. Coconut palm trees dominated the landscape, but the tour didn't stop there.

They stopped at archaeological sites, ancient stone temples and an American World War II site with several naval cannons. It gave a panoramic view of the island, and Kayla couldn't resist taking tons of photographs of the dazzling lagoon below.

"Who knew Tahiti had so much history?" Kayla wondered aloud as she snapped a photo.

"History wasn't the reason I chose this place."

"Well, of course not," Kayla returned. "You wanted a romantic, secluded location to seduce me, and you got your wish."

Ethan's brow rose. "Seduce you? I don't think I had to do

too much seducing. We both wanted each other, and without all the distractions of home, we could give in to our attraction."

"You're right. We certainly have no problem in the bedroom." Kayla turned around to take another picture.

"And I take it you think that's all we have or can have?" Ethan inquired, peering at her.

Kayla spun around. "Do you really want to have this discussion?" she asked. "Let's just enjoy our last few days here, okay?" She patted his arm. "And worry about tomorrow later."

Ethan surveyed Kayla's face. Now was not the time to bring up that it was possible they could have a real marriage in time, because Kayla was not open to the idea. Ethan walked toward her with his arms open so she could come to him. "No, we don't have to talk about this now, but there will a come a point that we will have to address this."

"Not now," Kayla said, standing on her tiptoes and brushing her lips across his.

The caress of Kayla's lips on Ethan's mouth made his body ache with need and had him forgetting all about a talk.

After two days of being on the go, the following day Kayla and Ethan had a leisurely day in and out of bed. They made love, sunbathed and swam in the ocean. Eventually, Ethan even whipped up some food in the kitchen so they wouldn't have to go to the hotel.

Time was passing quickly, and before Kayla knew it, they were on their last day in Bora Bora. They decided to spend part of the day at the resort spa. They started first with an open-air exotic foot bath and body polish followed by a couples' massage with hair and scalp treatment. The experience ended with a splendid tropical fruit smoothie.

Kayla couldn't have asked for a better end to their week-long honeymoon. "So what are we going to do on our last night?" Kayla asked, sipping on her smoothie.

"Make love until dawn." Ethan answered quickly.

Kayla smiled. "Besides that."

"I thought we would end our stay with a romantic candle-light dinner on the beach," Ethan said. "I've arranged for a boat to pick us up from our terrace at the villa and take us to a secluded beach where the resort staff will be on hand to serve us the finest Polynesian delicacies."

"I'm impressed." Kayla clapped her hands. "Did you leave anything up to chance on this honeymoon?"

Ethan looked at her long and hard. "Some things."

Kayla dressed to impress on their last night on the island. She'd curled her hair until the tresses fell in soft waves around her face. Ethan would salivate when he saw her in this shimmery concoction with plunging V-neck and front slit that came to her thigh. Ever since that night at the premiere, she'd enjoyed showing a little leg. Luckily the dress only reached her calves, so it would be easy to get in and out of a boat.

The dress was probably a bit much for a night on the beach, but Kayla wanted their last night to be special because it marked the last time she could just be herself with Ethan. While she was here, she'd been able to live her fantasy and immerse herself in Ethan. While she was here, she was free to express how she felt about him, if only physically. While she was here, she could forget about how she came to be Mrs. Ethan Graham.

But once they were home, everything would change. Once they were back, she would no longer be able to deny the fact that Ethan had coerced her into this marriage and although he desired her greatly, he didn't love her. She would no longer be able to deny that he'd used her to get her father's company.

Adams Cosmetics was part of Graham International, lock, stock and barrel. Kayla had no idea how she would handle the adjustment or exactly what Ethan's expectation was of her or her family. He'd been surprisingly quiet on the subject during the weeks leading up to the wedding. His absolute focus had been on making it the event of the year, so that Kayla feared what awaited her on the other side of the ocean.

"You ready, baby?" Ethan said, peeking his head into the bathroom where Kayla was finishing up getting ready.

Ethan stopped short in the door. "Wow! You look sexy as hell in that dress."

"I thought you might like it," Kayla said.

"You were holding out on me?"

"I saved the best for last, so let's do this."

A uniformed chauffeur picked them up outside the deck of their villa. Kayla walked along the plank and the chauffeur helped her inside the boat. Ethan hopped in and they were on their way.

The ride over to the resort's islet was short and sweet. Kayla had no idea what to expect, but she was surprised when they got there. They were taken to a secluded stretch of white sandy beach and palm trees, but right in the middle of it all was a covered cabana. Kayla wondered what awaited her inside.

After the chauffeur helped her off the boat, he said to Ethan, "I will be back for you in a couple of hours."

Ethan grasped Kayla's hand and together they walked to the cabana. Another uniformed waiter greeted them at the entrance. "Welcome, Mr. and Mrs. Graham," He held open the curtain for them. "I will be your server for the evening."

"Pleasure to meet you." Kayla smiled at him.

"You will love the dinner we've arranged for you this evening. It's a mixture of grilled lobster, gambas, lagoon fish, coconut rice and fresh fruits right here from Bora Bora."

"Sounds divine." Kayla glanced around, and the inside of the cabana was straight out of a Saharan movie. She half expected a sheikh to come walking through the tent. The sand had been covered with large damask rugs, so they wouldn't get sand in their toes. In the center was a candlelit table for two complete with fine champagne in a bucket of ice. Near the side were dozens and dozens of pillows of various colors and shades they could relax on after dinner. Soft music was coming from what Kayla could only imagine was a hidden jukebox.

"Look up," Ethan pointed to the ceiling so Kayla could see that a portion of the cabana was removed so they could see the stars at night.

Kayla shook her head in bewilderment. "This is truly incredible, Ethan. You thought of everything."

"Nothing but the best for you, Mrs. Graham." Ethan bent down to give her a kiss on the lips. It was soft and tender and not unlike the hundreds of others he'd given her over the week, but for some reason, Kayla felt like there was something more behind it. But she brushed it off. She wouldn't let her imagination run away with her just because Ethan knew how to romance a woman.

"Allow me." The waiter pulled out a chair at the table for Kayla.

"Thank you."

He then held out the other chair for Ethan. "Would you both care for some champagne?" the waiter inquired.

"We would love some, thanks," Ethan responded.

Kayla was surprised when Ethan grasped both her hands from the other side of the table. He had an intent look on his face, like he was about say something important, but the waiter handed them a flute of champagne each.

"You can begin serving the starter," Ethan said, "in about ten minutes." The waiter nodded before leaving the tent.

"What were you going to say before?" Kayla asked. Ethan was silent for a short while and Kayla wondered what was on his mind. "Whatever it is, Ethan, you can tell me, okay?" He was making her nervous.

"When we get back…" he began.

"Things will change."

"They don't have to," Ethan returned quickly. "Hasn't this week shown you that we're good together? We're a good team, Kayla. I know we can find common ground, in and out of bed."

"Ethan…" But he silenced her by reaching out to put his index finger against her lips.

"Let me finish," he said. "I know it's going to be an adjustment what…with your moving to my house and away from your family and even more so at the office."

Kayla's eyes grew big. *Okay, here it comes, she thought. He's going to tell me how to run Adams Cosmetics.* He'd only given lip service to the press when he'd said she'd still be at the helm.

"There will be some changes, Kayla. There have to be, but I can promise you that I will always consult you first."

Now that she hadn't expected.

"You're my wife, so I will give you that respect. All I ask in return is that you do the same."

"What do you mean?"

"I know your family hates me."

"Hate might be a strong word."

Ethan let out a hearty chuckle that could probably be heard outside the cabana. "C'mon, Kay." He used her nickname. "Do you think I'm blind? Your family is against me. It will be an uphill battle to win their respect."

"Which is where I come in?"

"Yes. At times you may have to be a mediator if you will. I just want peace and harmony at home and in the office. Adams Cosmetics won't get back on the map if we're at each other's throats."

Kayla nodded. "You have a point." Dissension among the ranks would only cause more strife.

"Then you'll have my back?" Ethan asked.

"I am no miracle worker, but I will do my best," Kayla answered honestly.

Ethan smiled. "That's all I can ask." He reached for his flute. "To our last night in paradise. Cheers!" Ethan clicked his flute against hers.

Their lovemaking that night was even more incredible, more passionate than it had ever been. Kayla didn't know if it was because of their talk over dinner or if it was just nostalgia because it was their last night in Bora Bora, but she was overcome with love for Ethan.

She nearly said she loved him when they'd come in a blaze of glory together, but she'd caught herself before she'd made a big fool of herself. No sense it putting herself out there and having Ethan stomp on her heart. He'd vowed to honor and respect her at work while of course keeping her satiated in the bedroom. What more could she ask for, right?

She could ask for *love,* for him to love her in return as much as she loved him. She'd thought she was besotted with the man when she was seventeen, but this was different. Becoming lovers had increased her feelings for Ethan tenfold, and Kayla was struggling with her love for him and her desire for self-preservation. She didn't want to get hurt.

She had to remember how they'd gotten here. Ethan had been willing to do anything and everything to get his hands on her father's company. Marrying and bedding her was an added benefit, she must never forget that. She must always endeavor to keep her feelings in check, because if Ethan found out, he could use them against her.

Chapter 10

"Welcome back, Kay," Shane said from the doorway of Kayla's office the following morning.

It had felt strange to Kayla to come back to Adams Cosmetics after the week-long whirlwind that was their honeymoon. It seemed like a lifetime.

She'd been even more unsettled when she'd woken up that morning and found Ethan already gone. Once they'd returned to his estate last night, they'd had a late supper and then Ethan had been eager to get her on her back as if to christen their bed.

Ethan had left a note that an emergency had come up overseas that he'd postponed for weeks but needed to address immediately at the office, but it still irked her. Kayla supposed she'd expected that they would spend a leisurely morning in bed making love and have breakfast together before going their separate ways at the office, kind of like in Bora Bora, but that had been far from the case.

"Shane." Kayla rose from her desk and rushed over into his arms. "It's good to see you." She kissed his cheek.

Shane stepped back to look at his sister. "You look really good, Kay. Very tan and very relaxed. I take it you had a good honeymoon?" He winked at her.

Kayla blushed. "I am not going to comment on my sex life with my little brother of all people," she said, and turned to walk toward the couch so they could catch up.

Shane followed behind her and joined her as she sat on the leather sofa. "You don't have to." He smiled knowingly. "We're both adults and this was a man you'd had a serious crush on for years. I *know* what happened."

Kayla rolled her eyes upward and ignored the statement. "Catch me up on AC." She shortened the name of the family business. "What's new? What have I missed?"

"Graham International sent some executives over to evaluate our processes."

"Is that right?" Kayla asked. She'd known they would come to see the lay of the land, but they'd done it while she'd been on her honeymoon? Was that Ethan's way of avoiding ruffling her feathers?

"And…" Shane smile grew even larger. "I have finalized the new fragrance."

"Shane!" Kayla patted his knee. "That's wonderful news and is by far the best wedding present I could get. In light of this merger, this couldn't come at a better time."

"I couldn't agree more. It's time to talk strategy."

"Is Courtney in?" Kayla asked, reaching for the phone.

"Now you know our little sister is off gallivanting in some part of the world, but she's due back in a couple of days."

"Well, we need to discuss our advertising campaign for this fragrance," Kayla stated, rushing over her desk. Before all the wedding shenanigans, they'd started some preliminary sketches. She looked at her calendar on her computer and threw out several dates to Shane.

"Any of those sound good to me," Shane said, rising from the couch.

"Let's shoot for tomorrow, then," Kayla said. "That'll give me a chance to get through all my phone calls and emails and then we'll get down to business."

"Welcome back in the saddle, kid!" Shane squeezed her shoulder. "We missed you!"

"And I've missed you," Kayla said, giving him a quick smile. She hadn't realized just how much until now.

Kayla waved to Piper when she saw her walk into the bistro café where they were meeting for dinner that evening.

"My gosh!" Piper exclaimed. "The bride has returned." She leaned across the table to give Kayla a quick hug. "And boy, does it look like you had a real good time."

Kayla laughed. "Piper, how are you, darling?"

"To hell with me," Piper said. "I want to know about you and that fine specimen of husband and why in the hell you're here with me on your second night back in town rather than in bed with your hubby."

"Wow!" Kayla's mouth formed into an O. "That's a lot to ask."

"I'm dying for the details. So leave nothing out."

Kayla laughed. "Well, we're having dinner tonight because said husband is working on a large deal and won't be home until later and told me to eat without him."

"And?"

"I presume you want to know about the honeymoon?"

"Uh, yeah…" Piper's green eyes grew large.

The waitress came over and interrupted them. "Wine?" she asked, looking at Piper. Since Kayla knew Piper's fa-

vorite she'd taken the liberty of ordering a bottle of her favorite red.

"Absolutely," Piper said, holding up her glass.

Once the waitress had filled her glass and gone, Kayla
leaned in. "We went to Bora Bora."

"As in Tahiti?"

Kayla nodded.

"Oh, my!" Piper leaned back with her glass of wine and
took a generous sip. "The man certainly knows how to romance."

"Even more." Kayla leaned forward. "We had a private
two-story villa on the lagoon with a deck and boat-docking
station. Piper, it was insane!" She tried not to raise her voice.
"And the sex, well…it lived up to every fantasy I'd ever had
and then some."

"Girl, stop!"

"I am not joking. Ethan was…no, make that *is* an amazing
lover. I think I had forgotten that part of myself, but Ethan
awakened my sexuality."

"Good for you." Piper chuckled and sipped on her wine.
"You probably needed it."

"Piper!" Kayla blushed.

"And so now…does this mean your marriage is real now?"

Kayla stared back at her best friend, unable to answer. It
caused Piper to place her wineglass on the table and stare at
her questioningly. "It's real for one of you, isn't it?"

Kayla nodded reluctantly. Maybe if she didn't verbalize
it, it wouldn't be true.

"Oh, Kayla." Piper's head hung low for a minute. Then
she popped up. "So Ethan feels nothing for you?"

"He desires me," Kayla answered. "Other than that, I
don't know."

"Kayla, you just spent twenty-four hours, seven days a

week with the man and you don't know how he feels about you?"

Kayla blinked back tears, fighting to keep them at bay. She shook her head. "I mean he cares for me. Respects me, if that's what you're asking."

"I'm asking if he *loves* you," Piper replied.

The four-letter word Kayla was afraid to think about, much less say out loud. She shook her head furiously and Piper leaned over and patted her hand.

"It's okay. Maybe in time he will."

Kayla swallowed hard. "That's very optimistic of you Piper, but I'm a realist. I know why Ethan married me, and love wasn't one of those reasons." She finally said the word aloud. He'd already made a preemptive move by sending his troops to evaluate her company without her. What was next?

"I pray that isn't true, Kayla. Otherwise you're in for a world of hurt."

Ethan was disappointed when he arrived home and found Kayla asleep. He'd hoped she might have waited up for him, but he guessed that it was pretty hard to ask, seeing that it was well after midnight. He'd tried to handle the overseas problem as expeditiously as possible, but he'd encountered one hurdle after another. He hadn't wanted to begin their life together stateside like this. He'd wanted to help Kayla get acclimated to her new life and instead he'd missed their first morning and night together. Kayla must be furious with him and probably assuming that it was back to business, but that was far from the case.

Their time in Bora Bora had meant a great deal to him, and he was becoming more attached to her than he had ever thought possible. He'd felt a connection between them when they were younger. The way Kayla looked at him with such adoration, it had been impossible to ignore. And he had to admit, he'd been flattered to be the object of her affection, but as she'd blossomed into a young woman he'd begun to desire her. It was then that he'd thrown himself into work and other women to exorcise her from his mind. It hadn't worked, and now he was facing an unfamiliar emotion. Could it be love?

He certainly didn't know how to love someone, at least not someone like Kayla. She would demand all of his heart and he wasn't sure he could give it. Sure, he'd loved his mother dearly, but that was as close to love as he'd ever gotten. Carter Graham hadn't wanted love. He wanted money, power and respect, and so Ethan had gone on the path of getting those things so that Carter would respect him, but Carter never offered up any praise. He was definitely nothing like Byron Adams, which was why it pained him that he was at odds with Kayla's father. Ethan respected Byron a great deal and hoped he would one day realize he wasn't Carter Graham incarnate.

Ethan bent down to kiss Kayla on the forehead as she slept. He would love to have her wake up to him making love to her body, but he would let her rest. There was always tomorrow.

When Kayla woke up the next morning, she was not alone, nor was Ethan asleep, because she could feel the thickness of his erection against her stomach. He was already looking down at her, his eyes ablaze with desire. "Good morning," she whispered, rubbing the sleep from her eyes.

"Good morning, wife," Ethan murmured. "I apologize for not giving you a proper send-off yesterday before you went to work."

"I understand…business sometimes takes a priority," Kayla responded groggily.

"Hmm…well, allow me to rectify that," Ethan said, and seconds later, his head was dipping underneath the covers.

He removed her panties so quickly, Kayla didn't have a moment to react as she was barely awake. Ethan kissed her belly, the soft flesh on her thighs and then he blew on the springy curls at her thighs. Kayla held her breath waiting in delicious anticipation of what was sure to come. So when Ethan spread her legs wide and began to tongue her with feverish delight, she cried out.

"Ohmigod!" Kayla moaned aloud. He used his tongue to make figure eights while he used his fingers to further exacerbate the tiny nub of her womanhood and bring her to a heightened sexual peak. Ethan grabbed her buttocks and brought her even closer to his hot, waiting tongue.

An orgasmic cry escaped her lips when he shifted to find her G-spot and worry it relentlessly with his tongue. A tidal wave swept her out to sea and she collapsed on the pillow when the second orgasm washed over her.

Ethan pulled back the covers, lifted his head and asked, "Am I forgiven for yesterday?"

Kayla was thinking about said orgasm as the advertising meeting was underway. She knew she should focus on the task at hand because it was critical to Adams Cosmetics getting back on track. It was just hard to do when her husband had just given her the best oral sex she'd had in her life.

Their head of advertising was talking about a concept that Courtney, who'd yet to make it back from Europe, would handle when Ethan came bursting through the door. Everyone suddenly jumped up as if their hands had been caught in the cookie jar.

"No need to rise, everyone, and I apologize for just barging in," Ethan said smoothly. "But I wasn't aware there was a meeting today." He turned to glare at Kayla and she could feel all eyes in the room on her.

"Would you mind excusing my wife and me while we speak? We'll reconvene in fifteen minutes."

Clearly, everyone knew who Ethan was and scurried out of the room, but Shane stayed behind to protect his sister from Ethan's wrath. He didn't like the way Ethan was glaring at her.

"We weren't trying to exclude you," Shane began, but Ethan held up his hand.

"I would like to speak with Kayla alone, please," Ethan said again, never taking his eyes off his wife.

Shane looked at Kayla, giving her a silent promise that he would stay if she needed him, but Kayla shook her head, so Shane headed to the exit.

Once the door closed, Ethan tore into Kayla. "How could you not tell me about this meeting?" he asked with a raised voice. "Especially after this morning?"

"Why should I?" Kayla's voice matched his. "I still run this company, or did that change when your cronies began raiding my company during our honeymoon? Matter of fact, how did you know about this meeting? Did you install some spies, too, while you were at it?"

"One, they are not cronies, they are members of my Acquisitions team and assess all my acquisitions to see what is or is not viable. Second, they didn't raid anything. Adams Cosmetics is exactly how you left it, at least for now."

Kayla was livid and she noted he didn't deny adding spies. "Oh, I see—you're going to dismantle us, 'your acquisition.'" She made quotation marks with her fingers.

"Damn it, Kayla." Ethan loosened his tie. "Why must you

jump to the worst possible conclusion? I'm not dismantling AC, but there are going to have to be changes to keep this company solvent. And one of them is Shane's fragrance. It's vital to relaunching Adams Cosmetics, and at the very least I should have been included in this meeting."

"Am I or am I not still running this company?" Kayla jumped to her feet as she yelled at Ethan.

"You are, with stipulations," Ethan said through clenched teeth. He hadn't wanted to get into this just yet, but clearly he didn't have much choice.

"Now...we get to the heart of the matter."

"As head of Graham International, all major decisions need to be run by me first." Ethan turned to his wife. "This fragrance—" he pointed to the mockup "—is one of them."

Kayla rolled her eyes. "So I'm just a figurehead." Bitterness was laced in her voice. "To the public I'm the CEO, but yet I'm not really, because you've cut off my feet. Is that what this morning was about? You were trying to get me all ready. To hell with you, Ethan!"

Kayla stormed out of the conference room and past several onlookers. Once she got to her office, she slammed the door and locked it. She slumped against the door and her head fell to her hands she cried. *What had she gotten herself into?*

Ethan continued the meeting with the advertising executives without Kayla. He would give her time to calm down and then go back to speak with her. This was the first true test of the marriage. He'd known it would come eventually, but didn't think it would be so soon.

When the meeting was over he walked to Kayla's office. Ethan knew she was angry with him, and it was about to get a whole lot worse once she heard his ideas for the fragrance advertising campaign.

"Is she in there?" he asked Myra.

"Yes, but the door is locked, as Kayla doesn't want to be disturbed when she's trying to help an employee."

"Is this something that Kayla does frequently?" Ethan inquired.

Myra nodded. "If anyone in the company needs help, they know they can always go to Ms. Adams and she will try and find a solution to whatever problem they may have."

So that's what Kayla meant by saying her employees were like family. Ethan was impressed at Kayla's generosity. Ethan doubted he'd ever inquired about an employee's life outside of work, other than the niceties. "I appreciate the info, Myra, but I need to speak with her. So if you can give me the key, please. And it is Mrs. Graham now."

"Of course." Myra was clearly flustered at her error and colored. "I apologize, Mr. Graham I'm just getting used to the name change."

"No problem, Myra. The key, please."

Reluctantly, Myra opened a drawer, pulled out a key and held it out to Ethan.

When Kayla looked up and saw Ethan standing in her doorway, she was furious. She was in a delicate meeting with one of the cafeteria cooks and had asked not to be disturbed.

Kayla pressed down her intercom. "Myra, I asked to be left alone. Phyllis, I am so sorry, we will finish this discussion on your next break, okay?" She apologized to the cook and rose from her desk to pat her hand as she escorted her to the door. "We'll figure something out."

"Don't be angry with Myra," Ethan said once the elderly woman had left. "I strong-armed her to give me the key."

"Figures." Kayla returned to her desk.

"I am not leaving until we talk about what happened today," Ethan said, coming to stand in front of her.

"You'll be waiting a long time," Kayla said. She picked up her phone to make a call, but Ethan grabbed the receiver out of her hand and slammed it down.

"I will not be dismissed by my wife," he returned testily.

"Oh, did I hit a nerve?" Kayla looked up at him. She knew she had. During their honeymoon, Ethan had mentioned how he'd hated when his father had ignored him. He would throw a tantrum, desperate for his attention, but Carter would merely call the nanny or his mother and have him removed.

"Well, imagine how I feel." She touched her chest. "You called me out and embarrassed me in front of my staff. And from what *my* spies tell me, you went ahead with the meeting without me."

Ethan breathed in deep and willed himself to calm down. He'd never known a woman who could get under his skin quite like Kayla could. He'd had no intention of losing his cool, but she'd riled him up by ignoring him. He hated that feeling because it reminded him of the way his father used to ignore him as a child.

"I'm sorry," he said finally. "I should not have done that, but I was taken aback to find you'd called a meeting this important without me. I went ahead with it because time is of the essence. Adams Cosmetics is hemorrhaging money and I've got to put a tourniquet on it. Shane's fragrance and potential line of fragrances has real promise and has to be handled right."

When Kayla didn't speak, Ethan continued, "It's why I

think the entire perfume line should be something unique and distinct from the cosmetics division."

"I'm listening…what aren't you saying?"

"There will be a new spokeswoman for the perfume line," Ethan stated.

"Excuse me?"

"The perfume line will have its own spokeswoman."

"Absolutely not!" Kayla stood up. "Courtney has always been the Adams Cosmetics spokeswoman. What are you trying to pull here, Ethan? You've already tying my hands. Are you trying to systematically get rid of every member of the Adams family out of Adams Cosmetics?"

"That's harsh, Kayla. I'm not getting rid of Courtney. I just think we should keep her on the cosmetics division."

"You should leave!" Kayla pointed to the door.

"Kayla, we need to talk about this."

"I can't talk to you, because you're talking nonsense. I can't believe you'd do this to my family." Kayla sighed. "Just go."

"Kayla, I respect your right to disagree with me, but my decision on this is final."

Kayla laughed bitterly. "You promised to 'consult me' in Bora Bora. This isn't consulting me, Ethan. This is telling me, but I guess since you're the majority shareholder I have no vote, so we have nothing left to say," she replied, and picked up her phone to make a call.

"Is everything all right?" Daniel asked Ethan when he found him still working late at Graham International's offices.

When Ethan glared at him, Daniel knew it wasn't, and closed the door behind him. He walked over to Ethan's wet bar and pulled out a bottle of scotch. He poured him and Ethan a glass.

He returned to Ethan's desk and set the glass on his desk. Ethan grasped it and chugged it down in one shot.

"All right," Daniel said. "You want to tell me what's going on?"

"That woman is so infuriating." Ethan ran his hands over his head.

"Oh, really?" Daniel laughed. "Did something happen?"

"Kayla pushed my buttons is what happened," Ethan answered. "She planned an advertising meeting on her brother's new fragrance line without including me."

"Isn't that one of the reasons you bought Adams Cosmetics?" Daniel asked. "Aside from other reasons," he added. He was no fool and knew Ethan was attracted to his wife.

"Absolutely. Shane Adams is one of the best chemists out there and I know this fragrance will be a slam dunk if handled properly."

"And Kayla doesn't agree?"

"Not when I told her that any major decisions concerning AC need to be run by me first." He should have made it clear to her sooner, but Kayla had to know that things wouldn't continue at Adams Cosmetics as they had been before the merger.

"Ah, there's the rub." Daniel rubbed his goatee thoughtfully.

"She was even more furious when I told her that I want a new spokeswoman for the perfume line."

"What's wrong with Courtney Adams? She's a beautiful woman."

"Agreed." Ethan nodded. "And she will still be the model for the cosmetics division, but I have someone else in mind for the perfume line."

"Oh, yeah? Who?"

"Noelle Warner."

"The actress you dated? Do you think that's a wise idea?" Daniel inquired. Noelle was one of Ethan's many exes.

"Noelle is the most celebrated actress on the planet after that Oscar this year, plus we've been through for a long time. She's dating that NFL player," Ethan commented. Noelle had always been one of the few women who understood the score when he said he wasn't looking for commitment. "Noelle has the right amount of innocence and sexiness to pull off the advertising campaign we've discussed. Start the discussions with Noelle's camp."

"Does Kayla know about you and Noelle?"

Ethan shook his head. He and Kayla had never really discussed their past relationships. He only knew what was in the dossier, and it was better that way. If he had to think of another man touching his wife, he'd blow a gasket.

"No. And why should it matter? Noelle and I were over long ago. Kayla couldn't possibly be threatened by her."

"I have to strongly discourage you on this, Ethan. You're playing with fire by underestimating an ex," Daniel warned. "And you will get burned."

Chapter 11

"He wants to take Courtney off the campaign?" her father said when Kayla came home after work instead of going to Ethan's home in Tuxedo Park.

"Yes." Kayla nodded as the family sat down and shared a cocktail before dinner. She couldn't bear to go home and sit down to a meal with Ethan. Not when she was still so furious with him.

"Why would he want to do that?" Shane asked. "Courtney is gorgeous."

"He said he wants to separate the two lines and make them more distinct," Kayla answered.

"But Courtney has always been the Adams spokeswoman. How can he do this?" her mother asked. "Courtney will not be happy."

"What will I not be happy with?" Courtney stood with her hand on her hip from the doorway. She was jetlagged after having returned from a trip to a fashion show in Paris. She always kept the Adams Cosmetics name fresh in people's minds. She'd even procured herself a walk in one of the designer's shows while she was there.

"Who's going to tell her?" Her mother looked at Byron, then Shane.

"Don't look at me." Shane shrugged his shoulders and looked at Kayla.

"Is someone going to tell me what's going on?" Courtney said, dropping her overnight bag on the floor with a thud and throwing herself in the oversize leather love seat across from Kayla. "Can someone fix me a cocktail? I'm parched."

"What no one wants to say," Kayla began slowly, heading to the wet bar to fix her sister a drink—which she would need, "is that Ethan has made his presence known at AC."

That information piqued Courtney and she sat straight up. "Oh, really? What has he done?"

Kayla fixed Courtney a cranberry and vodka and handed her the drink. Courtney took a quick sip and said, "Well, I'm waiting."

Kayla inhaled deeply and then just spit it out. "Ethan has informed me that all major decisions for AC have to be run past him and he has the final say. One of those decisions is he will be hiring a new spokesmodel for the perfume line."

"He can't do that!" Courtney said. "That's my area of the company." She had been the spokeswoman for nearly a decade, since she'd turned sixteen.

"He can and he will," Kayla stated.

"Why would he do this?" Courtney asked. "Does he think I'm not pretty enough?" She rushed over to mirror above the mantel to check her makeup. She turned from side to side, trying to find a flaw or a wrinkle, but she saw none. Even though she had brains to go along with her beauty, her face had always been the one way she could make a valuable contribution to the company. Hell, Shane had the lab and Kayla was the CEO. Where did that leave her?

Kayla rose from the couch and came over to stand behind Courtney. "You are stunning. This is Ethan's way of asserting his power of us, over me. This has nothing to do with you."

"How are you going to handle this, Kayla?" her father asked. He'd been surprisingly quiet about the whole scenario. She would have thought he would have been jumping up and down. Perhaps he knew it was a moot point.

"Honestly, I don't know, Daddy." Kayla turned around to face her family. "Ethan and I are at impasse on this. Because I will never agree with him and turn my back on my family." She reached over to squeeze Courtney's hand.

Kayla was quiet when she walked into the master bedroom hours later and found Ethan awake and perched against the headboard reading a book.

"Hello," Ethan said, but Kayla walked past him into her closet and began removing her clothes.

The more she'd thought about it on the drive home, the more she realized he must have had the idea for weeks, which is why he'd asked her to have his back with her family. But if this was his way of earning favor with them, he would be waiting a long time for their respect, much less their affection.

When she'd changed into her negligee, she went into the bathroom and began washing off her makeup. She was startled when she looked up in the mirror to find Ethan standing behind her.

"Is it your intention to give me the silent treatment, because you may have noticed I don't respond well to being ignored."

"That's too bad," Kayla returned, reaching for a hand towel and wiping her face, "because I'm not in the mood to fight with you, Ethan. It's been a long day."

"Neither am I, but I would like to know where you were this evening," Ethan replied. "You never called me."

"I didn't realize I had to tell you my whereabouts at every hour and every second of the day." Kayla reached for her moisturizer, poured a generous amount in her hands and began rubbing it into her face.

"God darn it, Kayla," Ethan hissed, slamming the book he'd been reading onto the counter. "Must you be so obtuse? It is common courtesy to let your husband know where you are so I don't have to worry."

Kayla turned to face him, her eyes clouded with fury. "I am not one of your acquisitions, Ethan. You don't rule me." She stalked out of the bathroom and headed toward the bed, but Ethan blocked her path.

"Are you purposely trying to rile me up?"

"I am not trying to *do* anything to you. Now move"

Ethan reluctantly stepped aside. "Listen, I'm sorry you're upset, but you must agree that we need to hash this out. We shouldn't go to bed angry." He didn't want to lose the closeness they'd shared during their honeymoon. It had the meant the world to him that she'd opened her heart to him in Bora Bora. It meant they were finally making progress toward having a real marriage. And now he was seeing it go up in flames, just as Daniel had warned.

"It will not be tonight," Kayla said, turning her back to him and walking to the bed. She hopped inside, pulled the covers up to her shoulders and leaned across to turn the lamp out over the nightstand. "Good night." Seconds later, her head hit the pillow, effectively ending their conversation.

Knock. Knock. "Come in," Shane said from the other end of the laboratory door. "Kayla, what are you doing here?"

"I needed to get away from my office," Kayla replied, pulling up a chair to watch Shane work.

"What's on your mind?"

"Have you seen the new mock-ups for the ad campaign for Hypnotic, the new fragrance?"

"I have," Shane replied, stopping what he was doing. "They're good."

"Yes." Kayla was quietly contemplative.

"So I take it things are no better on the home front?" Shane inquired, trying to read his sister.

"If you call being polite to each other better, then yes, we're doing great," Kayla replied sarcastically. She and Ethan had shared the same bed every night as per the terms of their marriage, but they had barely spoken over the past week.

Kayla had long since come to the realization that the decision of who was the spokeswoman was out of her hands. Adams Cosmetics was a subsidiary of Graham International now, and she had to answer to Ethan no matter how much she might dislike that fact. She'd had sacrificed her autonomy to keep the company solvent and she had to live with the consequences of her decision. She just didn't know how to mend fences with Ethan and she wasn't sure she should.

Yes, she loved him, but if things continued as they were, he would have to see that their marriage was a farce and let her out. Sure, AC would still be his, but she could still save face. It was much too hard to sleep next to him night after night knowing there would be nothing between them other than sex.

"One of you has to make the first move," Shane said, knocking her out of her reverie.

"Why should it be me?" Kayla asked.

"Because Ethan had a point," Shane offered. "Graham

International did acquire us and we should have informed him. I guess we both were so used to running things our way that we left him out."

"You agree with him?" Kayla asked.

"I see both sides. I don't agree with him not allowing Courtney to continue as spokeswoman. Her face is synonymous with the brand, but yet we have to include him."

Kayla smiled. "Well, that's good to hear."

"I just can't imagine what it's like with the two of you at war. Both of you are so stubborn neither one of you wants to give in. That house must be cold as ice."

"It hasn't been a walk in the park," Kayla admitted.

"So tell him you'll agree to disagree and call it a day."

Kayla hated that Shane made so much sense. She knew he was right, but she hated to give in first. Ethan should apologize. "Thank you, brother dear." She slid off the stool to give Shane a kiss on the cheek and he pinched her nose.

"I only want the best for you," he said. "Go make up with your husband." He patted her on the butt and nudged her out the door.

"Mrs. Graham is here to see you." Ethan's assistant buzzed his intercom later that afternoon.

Ethan's dropped the pen he'd been writing with and his heart suddenly began pounding loudly in his chest. Kayla was here? He was surprised as hell. She'd been mad at him for well over a week and he had to admit it had taken its toll. He'd been snappy more than a few times at Daniel the last week, causing him to give him a wide berth. And he'd most definitely felt it in the bedroom, as they hadn't made love since that second morning back from their honeymoon.

The boardroom hadn't been any fun, either. Kayla had sat across from him at the advertising meeting earlier in the week to discuss the campaign and Noelle's involvement and she'd stared daggers at him the whole time. Ethan was sure everyone else in the room had felt her resentment, because he sure had. Now he wasn't sure what to make of her surprise visit. She'd come to him on his turf. What did it mean? *Was she ready to let bygones be bygones?*

Several minutes went by and his assistant rang him again. "Would you like me to send her in?"

Ethan pushed down the answer button. "Yes, of course. My wife is always welcome."

Kayla came strolling in, looking stunningly beautiful with her hair swept up in a French roll, wearing a sleek ruffled cardigan that began at the waist and reached all the way to her neck along with a pencil skirt that showed her impressive curvy figure but barely reached her knee. It made Ethan instantly want to ravish her right there, to pull every pin out of her hair until it hung in waves down her shoulders and to unzip that cardigan to reveal the soft swell of her breasts that he knew were lying underneath.

When Kayla reached his desk, Ethan exhaled. He hadn't realized he'd been holding his breath until she was standing in front of him. What was wrong with him? He hadn't had this kind of strong physical reaction to a woman since... since...well, never.

"Kayla." Ethan nodded his head.

"Ethan." Kayla smiled hesitantly.

They stared at each other for what seemed like an eternity until Ethan spoke first. "What brings you here?"

Kayla swallowed. "Well, I..." She'd come here for a truce per Shane's advice, but she wasn't necessarily sure of how to go about it. She looked down, twisting her hands.

Before she could utter another sentence, Ethan jumped out of his seat and pulled her into his arms. Without preamble, he plunged his hand into her hair, tilted her head to the right angle and plundered her mouth with a kiss. He pressed his hips into hers until they were chest to chest, belly to belly.

Kayla strained against him. He lifted her to meet his growing arousal, wanting her to be tight against him. Blood pulsed through Ethan and his temples pounded as fiery need coursed through him. Kayla smelled so good and tasted so right. Kissing Kayla supercharged all of his senses, and Ethan couldn't get enough.

The soft sounds she made made him want to reach down under the hem of her skirt and feel the hot core of her at his fingertips, but he realized where he was and slowly eased away from Kayla. Her eyes were still closed and her mouth was still slightly open.

"I've missed you," Ethan whispered, brushing his lips over hers again.

Kayla's eyes popped open just then and she murmured, "I've missed you, too."

"Are you sure you're okay?" Kayla asked Courtney when her sister came down late one afternoon to watch Noelle Warner take some test shots for the new advertising campaign. They hadn't spoken much in the past couple of weeks, and Kayla suspected why. Courtney must blame her for Ethan choosing Noelle.

"Of course," Courtney returned testily.

"I know how difficult this is. And I'm sorry for any part I played in Ethan's decision," Kayla said with her arms folded across her chest.

"It's not your fault."

Kayla didn't think so. It was a hard transition for her to have to run her decisions by Ethan. She'd run Adams Cosmetics for nearly five years since her father had retired and wasn't used to having to answer to anyone.

She and Ethan had settled on having a once-a-week meeting to discuss any vital AC business. It was her compromise on keeping him informed on day-to-day operations.

Hiring Noelle was Ethan's decision. She was a beautiful woman, Kayla was sure, but she wasn't Courtney. She knew her sister was putting on a stiff upper lip, but it had to hurt having the one area where she made an impact on the company suddenly minimized by an outsider.

"She is stunning," Courtney admitted, looking at the actress. "I mean look at her bone structure. I could never have her figure unless I starved myself."

"Stop it, Courtney." Kayla circled her arms around her sister's waist. "I would kill for your size-four figure." At a size ten, Kayla was certainly considered curvy by industry standards. "You're gorgeous, and don't you ever forget it."

"If you'll excuse me." Courtney pulled away just as Ethan walked into the room. She gave him the evil eye on her way out.

"Hey, babe." Ethan kissed Kayla on the cheek.

"Hi."

"Your sister isn't too happy with me, is she?"

Kayla gave him a sideward glance. "Can you blame her?"

Ethan looked forward and watched Noelle sashay across the floor with ease. She was moving like a cougar. "Noelle is doing a great job."

"She's okay," Kayla commented. She didn't want to admit that she was uneasy around a woman as beautiful as Noelle. Noelle carried herself with an air of entitlement that frustrated Kayla because she probably was used to men falling at her feet. Even Ethan, standing beside her, seemed entranced by the actress.

"She'll do a fine job launching the fragrance line."

"If you say so."

Ethan stared down at Kayla. "You just refuse to admit that I could be right about this."

"The decision has been made and I've accepted it. What more do you want?" Kayla asked, peering at him.

"Nothing, I guess," Ethan returned. It was clear they were never going to agree on the subject. "Well, I have to get out of here. I will see you later for dinner?" He asked it as more of a question because he wasn't sure what mood Kayla would be in after the photo shoot.

"Yes."

"Great." Ethan bent down and kissed her soft lips. "I'll see you at home."

Even when she felt cross toward him, the barest brush of his lips on hers always evoked a response from deep within her belly. Kayla hated that her body was so traitorous when her mind wanted to keep him at bay.

Once Ethan walked away, Kayla noticed that Noelle was staring at them. She quickly looked away once she realized she'd been caught and returned to the task at hand, showing off her beautiful face.

When the photo shoot was done, Kayla thanked the photographer for a job well done. "It's always a joy to work for Adams Cosmetics," he said. "You're one of my favorite customers."

"And we love you, Jacques," Kayla replied. "I can't wait to see the films."

Jacques turned and glanced at Noelle, who was behind a screen getting undressed. "She was a natural."

Kayla signed off on some paperwork and was about to head back upstairs to her office when Noelle stopped her. "You're Kayla Adams, right?"

Kayla glanced up at the statuesque actress who towered over her by several inches. Up close, Noelle was even more stunningly beautiful. Her beautiful café-au-lait skin was flawless, and makeup only added to her natural beauty. And she was as thin as Courtney said, because she made Kayla feel uneasy at size ten. "I am. May I help you?"

"I just wanted to thank you and Ethan in person for this great opportunity."

"You're welcome." Kayla stepped away to leave, but Noelle's next words stopped her in her tracks.

"You will give Ethan my regards?"

Kayla spun around on her heels to face Noelle. "Excuse me?"

Noelle smiled. She'd hit her target. "Ethan and I go waaay back."

The inference left little doubt in Kayla's mind that Ethan and Noelle were not strangers. They'd been lovers.

"It's just so wonderful of him to use me to launch this new fragrance," Noelle gushed. "It will be a big boost to my career. So you absolutely must give him a big kiss for me."

Kayla's eyes narrowed. "Oh, I absolutely will."

When Ethan arrived home, Kayla was in the living room with her legs tucked underneath her and a drink in hand. "Started without me?" He asked, heading to the wet bar to pour himself a scotch.

"Something like that," Kayla answered curtly.

Ethan's head popped up when he heard a distinct tone of derision in Kayla's voice. "Is something wrong, my dear?" he asked, pouring a generous sum of scotch in the glass. He took a sip and headed over to the couch where Kayla was sitting and sat down beside her.

Kayla gave him a cursory glance. "Why would you say that?"

"Hmm…I don't know. Something in your tone perhaps?"

Kayla sipped on her drink. "I had a very interesting conversation today."

"Oh, yeah? With whom?"

"Noelle," Kayla answered.

Instantly, Ethan knew the direction this conversation was about to turn. "Kayla…"

Kayla turned to glare at him and put up her hand to stop him from speaking. "She wanted me to give you her regards and a big kiss, seeing as how you two go waaay back."

"I know you're upset."

"Upset?" Kayla laughed. "Upset that you didn't want my sister as the spokeswoman for Hypnotic, but you wanted your ex-girlfriend? Now why would I be upset about something like that?"

"When you say it like that it sounds sinister, like she's my mistress or something," Ethan responded. "And that's far from true."

"Oh, really?" Kayla raised a brow. "You could have fooled me."

"Kayla, listen." Ethan reached for her hand, but Kayla moved away farther on the couch.

"Why?" She hissed.

Ethan would try his best to explain. He and Kayla had finally found a happy medium and he didn't want to lose ground. They'd settled in like normal newlyweds and he had been enjoying wedded bliss. "Noelle and I haven't seen each other in five years, okay? I have no romantic interest in her, but she is a well-known actress who just won an Oscar. The exposure she can give us is off the charts."

"And why do you suppose she accepted this offer?" Kayla inquired, and then pointed at him. "You!"

"Noelle is dating an NFL player."

"So says the rumor mill," Kayla replied. She'd taken the liberty of going online and reading the gossip magazines on Noelle. She had quite the reputation for switching mates. She'd also come across images of her and Ethan together as a couple, which had only infuriated her further. "How could you not tell me this? Why did you let me get blindsided like that?"

"I'm sorry, Kayla, really I am, but Noelle and I were over long ago."

Kayla rolled her eyes upward. "I can accept that," she responded. "What I can't accept is you keeping secrets from me. I thought we promised to be honest with each other."

"Honestly, it wasn't my intention to be deceptive, and I'm sorry that you consider that I was."

Kayla eyed him suspiciously. She couldn't bear another argument between them. The last one had taken its toll. "Okay. I'm going to take what you're saying at face value."

"So I'm not in the doghouse?"

"Oh, you're still in the doghouse," Kayla replied. "So how do you intend to get yourself out?"

"Hmm…" Ethan rubbed his square jaw. "I can think of several ways." His eyes went to the V-neck sweater she was wearing in which he could see the swell of her breasts. "But how about this?" He pulled a small jewelry box out of his pocket and handed it to Kayla.

"When did you get this?" Kayla asked.

"On my way home. I knew you were upset about Courtney and I wanted to give you a little something to let you know that I was thinking about you."

Tears sprung to Kayla's eyes. "That was very thoughtful

of you." Ethan was surprising her more and more. Could they possibly have a real marriage, despite how it had begun?

"So are you going to open it?" Ethan inquired. He was happy that he'd finally done something right.

Kayla smiled and flipped open the lid. Inside was a beautiful three-pendant diamond necklace. "It's gorgeous." Kayla pulled it out of the box and laid it in her palm.

"Let me put it on you." Ethan reached over and took it out of her hand. Kayla turned around and lifted her head so Ethan could close the clasp around her neck.

When Kayla turned around, Ethan sat back to admire his handiwork. "It suits you."

"Thank you." Kayla leaned across the couch and kissed Ethan full on the lips.

Ethan lifted her off the couch with muscled ease. Kayla's soft luscious body slid against his and she got the full contact of how much he wanted her. Her mouth brushed his gently at first, but then she slowly deepened the kiss and he opened his mouth to her eager awaiting tongue. Her tongue stroked his with aching delight that awakened every fiber of his being. Their tongues dueled and Kayla gripped at his shirt as the onslaught of the kiss took her over.

Heat flooded through Ethan. He wanted her naked. When he reached for her breasts and began molding them over her sweater, Kayla whispered, "Let's take this to bedroom."

"What's wrong with right here?" Ethan said devilishly.

"Ethan, we have staff!" Kayla murmured. "Anyone could walk in."

And they would most definitely get an eyeful. Reluctantly, Ethan released her and sat them both up. "Spoilsport!"

"C'mon." Kayla pulled him off the couch. "Let's go upstairs."

Chapter 12

"The launch party for Hypnotic tonight is going to be off the charts," Ethan said as he and Kayla dressed to go to the party that evening. The advertising department had fast-tracked the photo shoot of Noelle and a commercial to ensure they could get Hypnotic in stores in time for the holidays. He was amazed at what they had accomplished in several weeks. Even more amazing were the small strides he'd made with the Adams family. He'd even attended their annual Fourth of July weekend in the Hamptons, something he hadn't done since his late teens. Though they hadn't spoken to him much, they had included him.

"I'm hoping it'll be a success." Kayla was excited, yet a little apprehensive about branching out into a new arena. She'd felt the same way when Adams Cosmetics had branched out to body washes, lotions, shampoos and conditioners, except this time she had the full support of Graham International's financial strength behind her.

"Are you concerned?" Ethan asked. He'd never seen Kayla express any doubt. She was still wearing her robe and putting on her makeup.

"I know Shane's put together a quality product," Kayla replied, adding a touch of blush to her cheeks, "but you never know how it's going to be received by the general public."

"The focus groups loved it," Ethan returned.

"True, but the Adams Cosmetics customer, although loyal, might be a little skeptical at first."

"Kind of like you were about the merger?" Ethan inquired.

Kayla merely smiled. She'd been more than a little skeptical about merging a corporate goliath like Graham International with her smaller company. She never wanted to lose the sense of family she had with her employees, but surprisingly they were getting along well.

"Apparently, I'm not the only skeptical one. We have others banking on us falling flat on our butts," Kayla returned.

"Oh, yeah?"

"I received a congratulatory bouquet at the office today from Jax Cosmetics."

"Considering the history with your father, that seems disingenuous."

"Exactly! Andrew Jackson is just waiting for us to fail, so he can rub it in my father's face. I'm sure he's hoping Hypnotic's launch is a disaster."

"Well, he will be wrong," Ethan responded. "I never lose. Are you almost ready?"

Kayla loved Ethan's confidence. Some might call it arrogance, but at times it was sexy as hell. "Just about."

"I don't want to be late to your parents'," Ethan replied. Ethan would have preferred to go separately with his wife and meet the Adamses at the launch party, but they had a tradition of attending every party as a family unit. And if he broke tradition, Byron Adams would have his head.

When Kayla emerged from the master bathroom, Ethan sucked in a deep breath. She was wearing a scarlet strapless dress with a tightly fitted bodice that fit her curvy body and flared out with a long train behind her.

Kayla liked what she saw as well and gave Ethan a catcall. He was standing tall in a classic black one-button tuxedo with satin collar, skinny satin tie and matching pants.

"Thanks, babe." Ethan smiled, "But nothing compares to you in that dress."

"Oh, this old thing?" Kayla lied. She'd spent a great deal of time finding the right dress. She and Piper had gone to several stores the past weekend trying to find just the right dress for the launch tonight.

Ethan offered his arm. "Ready to go?"

"Absolutely." Kayla grabbed her clutch purse sitting on the bed and they were on their way.

Her parents were in the great room as usual and waiting for Kayla when she and Ethan arrived. Her father was pacing near the mantel as he always did.

"Baby girl, you look beautiful as always." He kissed her on the cheek. He held both her hands and stood back to look at her. "You get more beautiful each time I see you."

Kayla blushed. "Oh, stop it, Daddy."

"Oh, no, please do fill her head," Shane said from the opposite side of the room. "She needs the praise." He loved teasing his big sister because he knew how much it irked her.

Kayla turned to her brother and made a face.

"All right you two," her mother said. "Play nice."

"Byron." Ethan held his hand out. That's when Kayla realized he was still waiting by the mantel to be acknowledged.

Her father glanced over at him. "Graham."

"Why don't you try calling him Ethan, Daddy?" Kayla offered. It was much less hostile than calling him by his last name.

"Very well," Byron said, turning to his daughter. "For you, I will. Ethan, thank you for bringing Kayla over. It's always been a tradition for us to attend Adams Cosmetics functions together as a family."

"It was pleasure as we are a family now," Ethan commented.

A loud "ahem" was heard from behind them and Ethan turned and found Courtney standing behind her. "Courtney, you're looking ravishing tonight."

Courtney stood with her hair done up like a princess in a white strapless gown with a ruffled organza bottom from waist to feet. A simple black tie sash was the only detail. "Apparently, not ravishing enough," she said underneath her breath as she passed by Ethan and walked into the room toward her sister.

"Kayla, it's good to see you, sis. We've missed you. Your time has been monopolized these days."

Ethan heard the first dig, but Kayla hadn't and she responded with, "I'm sorry. Let's plan on a game of tennis this weekend."

"Sounds good. So is everyone ready to go?" Courtney inquired, glancing around.

"Now that you've finally graced us with your presence," Shane said, laughing, "we are."

"Put a sock in it!" Courtney sniped back.

"I just love having the entire family together again," their father stated. "Everyone grab a glass of champagne." Half a dozen glasses were already waiting on a nearby table, thanks to Victor. The entire Adams family came forward and grabbed a glass.

Byron Adams held up his flute. "Let's go show the world that nothing can keep us down and we stand strong."

"To family." They all raised a glass.

The press snapped photos of the family as they exited the limousine and fired rapid questions at them left and right. "When will the perfume debut in stores? Is Adams Cosmetics working on another one?"

"Soon," Kayla answered the first question.

Shane followed with, "You'll have to wait and see."

Inside, the launch party was a huge success. The ballroom of the hotel where the party was being held was filled to capacity. All the major media outlets in Atlanta were present.

A prominent editor from one of the top women's magazines stopped Kayla. "I absolutely love Hypnotic," she gushed. "I think the fragrance will be a hit with our readers. You really must give a sample for an advertisement."

"Absolutely!" Kayla smiled and squeezed Ethan's hand at her side. From what she could tell, everyone loved Hypnotic. Kayla had heard only positive responses from both the media and the other guests.

Ethan and Kayla made the rounds, smiling at photographers, greeting guests and making small talk. Ethan never seemed to leave her side; he played the dutiful husband with his hand lightly on the small of her back, causing Kayla to wonder if he was developing genuine feelings for her.

When it was time for her to thank everyone for coming and introduce Hypnotic as well as their spokeswoman, Ethan stood beside her onstage along with the entire Adams family.

Ethan felt it only appropriate that she as CEO of Adams Cosmetics make the announcement.

"I would like to thank you all for coming tonight. I think I speak for the entire Adams family when I say that we are excited to have you here tonight. We're excited to debut Hypnotic to you first," Kayla said, microphone in hand. "It's a brand-new area for Adams Cosmetics that we think our loyal customers will love. We invite you to partake of the samples around the room. Heck, take some home with you and introduce it to your friends." She was wrapping up her speech when Ethan whispered for her to mention Noelle. "And of course, meet our new spokeswoman, Noelle Warner." Kayla motioned to Noelle, standing in the center of the room with a spotlight on her. "In the meantime, enjoy the delicious food and champagne we've had catered for tonight's event. To Hypnotic!" Kayla held up her champagne flute.

All the participants raised their glasses. "To Hypnotic!"

Ethan came over and gave Kayla the most public kiss they'd ever had. It caused the crowd to clap in ovation. "We are newlyweds, after all..." Ethan said into the mike.

Later on, when Kayla was getting some canapés, Piper rushed over to give her a big hug. "Girlfriend, I love it!" she gushed, smelling her wrists. "This fragrance is going to put AC back on the map."

"You mean it?" Kayla asked, putting down the small plate she'd been piling high with food.

"Of course I do!" Piper hit Kayla on the shoulder. "You know I would never lie to you. Shane has outdone himself."

A smile spread across Kayla's face. "Thanks, doll. That means a lot." Kayla plopped an hors d'oeuvre into her mouth. She was starved. Actually, she'd noticed her appetite had increased of late, but she suspected it was due to all the stress she was under, as she was an emotional eater.

"And Ethan...well, that kiss up there was hot stuff," Piper commented. "Seems like the two of you are on the right path."

Kayla nodded and put her hand over her mouth as she finished chewing. When she was done, she said, "We've come to a meeting of the minds."

"I'd say a meeting of the bodies," Piper chuckled.

Kayla blushed. "That, too."

"Have you told him how you feel?"

Kayla shook her head furiously. "Absolutely not. His knowing that I love him would change nothing and would only make it awkward between us. It is better I keep those feelings to myself."

"For how long?" Piper asked. "How long do you think you can keep up this ruse that you care nothing for the man, when you're sleeping and living with him day after day?"

"As long as it takes for Ethan to let me out of this sham of a marriage."

"Is that honestly what you want?" Piper inquired. "To be let out of the marriage? You love him!"

Kayla grabbed Piper by the arm and pulled her aside so no one could hear their conversation. "And he doesn't love me," she whispered. "So can we drop this? No good can come from talking about this."

"No good?" Piper said. "I hate to spoil your night, Kayla, but you're bottling your feelings up inside and eventually they are going to erupt. And when they do, it won't be good."

"I won't let that happen."

"Oh, that's right. Strong, competent Kayla, always fighting to stay in control, right?" Piper asked. "Well, there are some things that even you can't control, Kayla. Like love."

"I can control it," Kayla responded. She had to, because if Ethan truly knew how she felt, he would have too much power over her. She couldn't allow that to happen.

"What are you so afraid of? Maybe he's feeling the same way about you. But you'll never know unless you take a chance and tell him how you feel."

The entire conversation was making Kayla uncomfortable and she had to make a quick exit. "You know what, I see someone I have to speak with," Kayla said, looking over Piper's shoulder at an imaginary person. "I must go say hello." And before Piper could object, Kayla was making her way through the crowd.

She passed by Shane, who was talking to a woman who appeared to be enraptured by his every word. Courtney, as usual, was talking to reporters, and her parents were seated at a table eating hors d'oeuvres. The only person she didn't see was Ethan. Kayla continued searching the crowd for her husband.

Ethan was speaking with a colleague on the terrace of the hotel when Noelle approached him.

"Noelle, you're looking well," Ethan said when she joined him. He gave her a hug and tried to pull away quickly, but she held on a little longer than he expected. "How are you, my dear?" He tried to sound lighthearted.

"Ethan, it's been a long time," Noelle replied. "Where have you been hiding yourself?"

"What do you mean?"

"You've been suspiciously absent of late at the photo shoot and then at the commercial for Hypnotic."

"My wife is CEO of Adams Cosmetics, Noelle."

"Oh, please," Noelle shushed him. "Everyone knows that's merely a formality and you're the real one in charge."

"No, it's not," Ethan challenged her. "Kayla is in charge."

"Really?" Noelle raised an eyebrow. "So she chose me to replace her sister as spokeswoman for this campaign? I don't think so."

"You just won an Oscar, Noelle," Ethan replied, smiling and catering to her ego. "You're hot right now, and we're capitalizing on that."

"Clearly, but that's not why I accepted this job."

"And why did you?"

Noelle slid closer to Ethan and tugged his tie. "You, of course, silly." She came forward until her lips were inches from his. "I wanted to see if we could rekindle the past."

"Noelle." Ethan looked down at her. "I am a married man."

"And I'm seeing Mitch Blake," she responded. "But that doesn't mean anything. What they don't know won't hurt them."

From the other side of the terrace behind the bushes, Kayla fell back against the building, completely floored. Although she couldn't hear their conversation, Noelle was cheek to cheek, hip to hip with Ethan and he didn't seem to mind. It was clear they were carrying on an affair right under her nose. *How could she have been so blind?* Ethan had no intention of ever making this a real marriage. He'd used her to get her father's company probably as a way to right an old grudge between their fathers, and she'd been caught in the middle.

And to make matters worse, her "husband" was cozying up with their spokeswoman where any passerby could see them. It was humiliating, and Kayla couldn't stand to watch it another minute. She wanted to go over and confront them both, but what purpose would that serve but to mortify her even further? Though she doubted it was possible to sink lower than she felt at this moment.

With leaden feet, Kayla forced herself from bushes she'd crouched behind, brushed herself off and went back into the launch party to salvage what she could of the evening. Adams Cosmetics would be a success despite Ethan Graham.

"Listen, Noelle." Ethan grabbed both Noelle's hands, which she'd been trying to circle around his neck, and pushed her away. "I'm not interested in *rekindling* anything with you. Ours is a professional relationship only. I'm sorry if you got the impression that there was more to this opportunity, but there isn't."

"Are you saying you're in love with her?" Noelle pointed to the ballroom.

Ethan stared in the direction of the party and then back at Noelle. Love? He'd certainly considered the idea before, but now that she'd said it, it sounded so real and probable. But even if he did love his wife, he was certainly not about to tell Noelle. He needed to sort out his feelings first. "That's none of your concern," Ethan finally answered. "All you need to concern yourself with is the Hypnotic campaign and nothing further."

Noelle shrugged. "If that's the way you want it. It seems like such a terrible waste. I doubt that prim and proper girl even knows how to please a sexual man such as you."

Ethan smiled to himself. That prim and proper girl more than knew how to please him, and he was already looking forward to the end of the evening. "Noelle, since we've known each other so long I'm going to let that slide, but don't ever speak about my wife in a derogatory manner again or you will not like the outcome."

"Fine!" Noelle pouted and then stalked off into the ballroom.

Ethan stayed out on the terrace for a moment longer to think about the question posed to him. Was Noelle right? Was he falling in love with Kayla? And if he were, how was he going to handle it?

"That was a long night," Ethan said in the limousine on the way home. It was nearly midnight and they were making they were way out of Atlanta and back into the outskirts of the city.

"Yeah, it was," Kayla said, rubbing her shoulders as she looked out the window.

Ethan leaned over and began massaging her shoulders. "You're tense as hell." He used his thumb and fingers to massage several pressure points.

Kayla was tense because Ethan, cheater that he was, was touching her, but what could she do? After she'd left him and Noelle on the terrace, she'd thought about her situation. She was in between a rock and a hard place. Ethan had her exactly where he wanted her. He had all the power. He'd forced her into this marriage and taken advantage of her unrequited crush to get her into bed, and to make matters worse he'd tired of her. He'd resorted to taking a lover, and what could she do?

He had majority interest in Adams Cosmetics. If she left him, there was no guarantee he wouldn't dismantle Adams Cosmetics and leave her and the family with nothing. She had to force him to let her go, but how? Of that she wasn't sure, but she would come up with a game plan to force his hand. There was no way Ethan Graham would get away with making a fool out of her.

Once they were back at the house, Kayla feigned illness.

"Is there anything I can do?" Ethan asked, concerned. She'd seemed fine earlier.

"No, I just feel like I'm coming down with something, so I'm going to sleep in one of the guest rooms," Kayla said with a straight face as she stared at her husband. "I wouldn't want you to come down with it."

"Don't worry about that," Ethan said. "I'm as strong as an ox." He didn't want to sleep alone. He'd rather gotten used to having Kayla by his side. Even when they didn't have sex, when he rolled over and felt her soft body, he was instantly comforted. And after Noelle's comments tonight, he wanted to be with her. He needed to be.

Kayla shook her head. "No, I think it's best." When he went to touch her forehead for a fever, Kayla pulled away. "It could be the flu or something, and don't you have the big meeting in a couple of days? You wouldn't want to get sick and have to cancel, would you?"

"I guess you're right," Ethan said reluctantly as Kayla began to walk down the hall to one of ten guest rooms in the mansion. "Are you sure you don't want me to tuck you in?"

Kayla turned around. "That won't be necessary." And seconds later, she was inside the safety of the guest room. Kayla leaned against the door. The sick card wasn't going to work for long. Ethan was a smart man and he would call in a doctor.

But after seeing him with Noelle, Kayla couldn't bear to have him touch her. The thought of him wanting to make love to her tonight made her physically ill. She'd come up with an excuse to have some time to herself so she could figure out a game plan. Ethan Graham may have beat her once, but he wouldn't again.

Chapter 13

"I'm sorry, Kayla, that I don't have better news," her attorney told her on Sunday morning. Since he was an old family friend, he'd graciously agreed to meet her on the weekend. Ethan was out playing golf and didn't know she'd sneaked out of the house, especially since she'd claimed illness and not slept in their bed the past two nights. "If you try to divorce Ethan, as the majority shareholder, he could cut you and the entire Adams family out of Adams Cosmetics. Your agreement is ironclad."

Kayla nodded. "Thank you, Alan. I appreciate you taking the time to explain things." She'd already known what he was going to say, but she guessed she had to hear it out of the horse's mouth. Then an idea popped in her head. "What if he divorced me?"

"What do you mean?"

"What if I had incriminating information that Ethan would never want leaked?" Kayla suggested.

"Then you might have some leverage to force his hand."

"Force him to give me back shares in a divorce?" Kayla asked. It would put them on equal footing.

"Smart girl." Alan nodded. "But I doubt Ethan will give in easily no matter how much leverage you had. He strikes as a man who doesn't like to lose."

Kayla rose from her chair. "We'll be in touch." She shook his hand on the way out. Now she had to get the proof that Ethan was unfaithful and then the gloves were coming off.

"You look contemplative," Daniel said after they'd just finished a round of golf with clients at their hotel and were standing outside waiting for the valet to bring Ethan's car round.

"What was that?" Ethan asked wistfully.

"I asked what you're thinking about," Daniel returned. "You've been off all day." Ethan had missed several easy shots, and they'd lost the game, which they never did. Ethan was an excellent golfer.

Ethan blinked several times and came back to the present. "Sorry, Daniel. I just have a lot on my mind."

"Oh, yeah? Is it something I can help with?"

"No, it's personal."

"Kayla?"

Ethan shook his head. "Noelle came on to me at the launch party the other night."

"I told you no good would come of having her back in your orbit."

"It's not that," Ethan said. "I told her I was married, but she said something that shook me to my core...had me thinking."

"What was it?"

"She asked me if I was in love with Kayla."

Now that gave Daniel pause and he turned to face Ethan. "Are you?"

Ethan glanced at him sideways. "Why would you ask that?"

"Because I've noticed how close you guys have been lately, so it does make me wonder."

"We're making the best of the marriage."

"Yeah, or you're falling in love with your wife. And if you are, there's nothing wrong with that," Daniel responded. "You started this marriage for business purposes, but it can turn into true love."

"No, it can't be love." Ethan shook his head. He'd come to the conclusion the other night that it had to be something else, because he was just too scared to face the prospect that it could be real. "I think it's just lust, plain and simple." Lust he understood. Love, he didn't know anything about love or how to go about showing it. Was Kayla thinking the same? He didn't want to give her any false hopes.

Daniel shrugged. "If you say so."

"Wow! I can't believe I have you all to myself," Courtney said when Kayla showed up for their game of tennis a week later. They'd decided on neutral territory and played several games at the country club. "I thought Ethan had locked you in that cave he calls an estate never to let you out again."

Kayla laughed. "It hasn't been that bad."

Courtney raised an eyebrow. "Are you kidding me? Everyone knows you two are newlyweds because no one ever sees you."

Kayla thought about that. The past few months, it had been work and home. With home being their bedroom, they'd been voracious for each other, until now. Now that she knew that Ethan was a cold-hearted bastard who was only in the marriage for power to control Adams Cosmetics. He needed the company to perk up his lackluster cosmetics division. When their father had left Graham International, he'd taken his creativity with him and they'd never recovered, which was why Ethan was so determined to have the company. And now that he was bored with sex with Kayla, it was on to Noelle.

"Well, I'm here now," Kayla said firmly. "And I promise to not let Ethan come between us again. My family means everything to me. You know I love you, don't you?" Kayla leaned over to give Courtney a hug.

Courtney looked at her strangely. "Are you sure you're okay?" She stared deep into Kayla's brown eyes trying to figure out what her sister wasn't telling her. "You played fiercely today. There was no way I was going to make a couple of those shots you sent my way."

"It was a good set."

"No, you killed it!" Courtney laughed. "Did you and Ethan have a fight and you have some inner aggression to unleash?"

When Kayla was silent for a moment, Courtney realized she hit the nail on the head. "Is all not smooth in paradise?"

"We've hit a bump in the road," Kayla replied. "And that's all I'm going to say on the subject. Today is all about us." She couldn't afford to let anyone else in on her plan. The element of surprise was crucial. Right when Ethan thought he had her, she'd show her trump card.

"Well, it's about time," Courtney said.

They were laughing when a familiar male figure came toward Kayla.

"Kayla Adams!"

"Ayden Turner!" Kayla replied. "Ohmigod, how long has it been?" she said, rising from her chair to give him a hug.

"It's been a while," Ayden replied, still holding her hands. "Let me look at you." He twirled her around with one hand and Kayla posed. "You look amazing."

"So do you." Kayla smiled warmly. Ayden had been her college sweetheart. They'd dated during her senior year and even after, when she obtained her MBA, but then a job opportunity led Ayden out of the country, and Kayla was never going to leave Adams Cosmetics and follow him because she was Byron's successor. Or so she'd told Ayden.

Time had aged Ayden perfectly. His caramel-colored skin had a warm hue and it looked like he'd packed on a few extra muscles in the past eight years because he was ripped in his jersey and tennis shorts.

"What are you doing in town?" Kayla inquired.

"I've been relocated back to Atlanta," Ayden returned.

"You have?" Courtney piped up.

That's when Ayden turned to acknowledge her as his attention had been solely focused on Kayla. "Courtney?" His voice rose several octaves. "Wow! Girl, you've sure have grown up."

Courtney's mouth widened into a grin. "Yes, I have."

"Gimme some." He came forward, lifting her off her feet into a hug.

"It's good to see you, Ayden," Courtney said. "Now put me down." Once he'd lowered her to her feet, she added, "You and Kayla should get together and catch up." She winked at her sister.

Kayla didn't like the hint of devilishness in Courtney's eye. "I am a married woman now." Kayla held up her seven-carat ring so Ayden could see.

"So? That doesn't mean two old friends can't catch up over a friendly drink." When Kayla frowned, Ayden said, "Okay, how about lunch tomorrow?"

Kayla smiled. "Lunch sounds good." Even though Ethan was a cheater, Kayla was a woman of her word and she didn't intend to betray her vows. They meant something to her.

"Okay, say one o'clock?" Ayden asked.

"Perfect!" They exchanged telephone numbers and Kayla saved his information in her cell phone. "I'll call you with a place."

"Okay, see you then." Ayden leaned down and brushed his lips across her cheek before leaving. "See you, Courtney."

"Bye, Ayden." Once he'd gone, Courtney turned to Kayla. "Can you believe that?" she asked. "You and the dictator are having problems and suddenly Ayden drops back into the picture? What are the odds?"

Kayla shook her finger at her sister. "I see your mind turning, and just stop it, okay? Ayden and I were through a long time ago."

"That may be so, but did you see how he was looking at you? You could still have a chance with a man you actually *loved*."

Kayla didn't comment because little did Courtney know that she was actually already in love, in love with lying, deceitful Ethan, a man who showed little regard for her feelings and who didn't love her, never had. "That's why I love you, Courtney, you and your vivid ideas on romance, but my fate has already been sealed." And soon it would be unsealed.

"Hey, babe." Ethan rose from the bed where he was reading to kiss Kayla when she walked into the master bedroom later that evening.

"Ethan." Kayla nodded and walked past him to go into the bathroom to shower. She was removing her tennis clothes when she noticed Ethan standing at the doorway watching her. She stopped and held her bra against her bare breasts. "What are you doing?"

"Just watching my wife undress."

"Oh." A lump formed in Kayla's throat and she turned around and continued taking off her clothes. She'd done her best to avoid sleeping with Ethan for over a week and she'd done a good job up until now. She knew the passionate look in his eyes. He wanted her.

When the last piece of clothing dropped to the floor, Kayla went to head to the shower, but out of nowhere, Ethan was in front of her. His eyes raked boldly over her. "I've missed you. I'm glad you're feeling better," he said, before gathering her naked body in his arms and lowering his head. His lips brushed hers softly, and then he pushed them apart. He slipped his tongue inside and merged it with hers while his hands roamed her backside.

Kayla needed to pull away, otherwise her body would betray what her mind knew to be right, which was he couldn't be trusted. "Ethan." She pushed him away. "I need to shower. I'm all hot and sweaty from tennis."

"Well, that's how we both can be, if you give it a chance." He went to lower his head again, but Kayla pulled away and reached inside the shower to turn on the taps.

"Not now." And before Ethan could say another word, she'd hopped into the shower.

When she emerged, Ethan was sitting at her vanity table. She wrapped the towel around her bosom and casually walked over to the sink counter to lotion her skin and add moisturizer to her face.

After several long, excruciating moments, Ethan finally asked, "Do you want to tell me what's wrong?" He'd been watching her body language and she was tense, which meant she was on edge about something.

"Wrong?" Kayla asked, rubbing the lotion into her skin.

"Don't play dumb, Kayla. It doesn't suit you."

"I don't know what you're talking about." She dropped her towel to the floor, reached for her robe on a nearby hook, wrapped it around her and tied the knot.

"I'm talking about the fact that we haven't made love in well over a week," Ethan responded with a hint of sarcasm.

"Oh, that." Kayla laughed. "Why are you making a big deal about it? I was feeling poorly. And married couples have lulls." Or so she'd heard. It sounded reasonable to her.

"We don't."

Kayla didn't have a smart comeback because he was right. Since their wedding and the week they'd been mad at each over about Hypnotic's new spokesmodel, they had made love every night or every other night. Ethan was staring at her from the vanity to her left, but Kayla refused to look at him, staring straight in the mirror and reaching for her hairbrush.

When she didn't respond, Ethan acquiesced and said, "If I've done something that you're upset about, just let me know and we can talk about it."

"So you can win?" Kayla asked calmly.

"No!" Ethan rose and came to stand behind her in the mirror. "Because I hate this distance between us, don't you?" He rubbed her shoulders, but she recoiled from his touch.

"Ethan, I'm really tired." Kayla brushed her hair. "And I am not in the mood to argue because you're horny and I'm not."

"That's not it at all, and you know it!" Ethan replied. His temperature was steadily rising, but Kayla appeared calm, and it infuriated him further. "Stop acting like I'm some horndog after your body. You like sex as much as I do."

"And I'm not in the mood, okay?" Kayla said, turning to face him.

"Don't dismiss me. I'm your husband."

Fury boiled inside Kayla. He had some nerve to talk about his rights as a husband. All he cared about was getting her into bed, not what was in her mind, in her heart. He was callous and unfeeling. "I'm well aware of that. And before you remind me of our agreement, I know my wifely duties, so go take a cold shower."

She stormed out of the bathroom and went into the closet to find a nightie. When she came out, Ethan was thankfully gone.

Kayla breathed a sigh of relief. If he'd pressured her or turned on the seduction, she wasn't sure she would have been strong enough to resist him. He had a way with his mouth and tongue that brought her to her knees, but apparently he wasn't interested in coercing a response from her.

Seconds later, she heard the roar of an engine in the distance. Ethan had left without a word.

Ethan made his way to one of his old stomping grounds to blow off some steam—the gentleman's club he and Daniel frequented before he'd gotten married.

It was somewhere he could let down his hair without being judged, and he desperately needed that right now. Kayla had worked his last nerve. She'd outright refused to sleep with him, and he was mad as hell because he didn't know why she was upset.

A strong drink was what he needed, and maybe a few more after that. Perhaps he could get over the sting of his wife's rejection.

Kayla woke up the next morning before daylight and Ethan's side of the bed was untouched, which meant he'd stayed out the entire night and never came home. Was he out with that harlot? How could he talk about her neglecting her wifely duties, when he was having an affair?

She dressed for work and made her way to the office. She was happy to get off the estate and to a place where she belonged, where she understood what was expected and could meet those expectations. Not a fake marriage, in which she felt used and useless.

As she was pulling her Porsche into her parking space, Shane was pulling in next to her at the same time. He jumped out of his car first and opened the driver's door for her. "A bit early for you sis, ain't it?" he asked, looking at his watch. It read 7:30 a.m.

"Not today, Shane." Kayla frowned.

"Care for a cup of coffee?" Shane inquired. "We could talk."

"Okay, I guess." Kayla leaned over to grab her briefcase and followed Shane inside the Adams Cosmetics building. Kayla greeted the security guard at the front desk and pressed the elevator call button.

"A bit anxious today?" Shane inquired.

"I didn't sleep very well," Kayla replied. Truth was she'd barely slept at all, tossing and turning because she'd been waiting for Ethan to return, and when he hadn't, around 3:00 a.m. she'd finally drifted off to sleep.

"Then a large coffee is definitely in order."

They stopped in the cafeteria first and Kayla grabbed a large coffee and blueberry muffin. Shane motioned for Kayla to join him at a nearby table where she began scarfing down the muffin.

"One, slow down," Shane said. "That muffin isn't going anywhere, and two, spill it. Whatever is going on with you, that is. You only eat like this when you're stressed. Matter of fact, since when do you like blueberries?"

Kayla glanced down at the remainder of the muffin on the plate. She picked another piece off the side. "Hmm…I don't know. It's a craving, I guess."

"So what's going on? And don't lie to me, you're obviously very unhappy and it breaks my heart."

Her head bowed and her body slumped over in despair, she couldn't talk about it. She'd made a horrible mess of things.

"Okay, since you won't talk, I will." Shane placed his hand over hers. "You're miserable in this marriage and you know what? I should never have let you go through with it."

Kayla shrugged in mock resignation. "Don't blame yourself. It was my decision. No one forced me."

"Didn't he? Ethan knew how much AC meant to you, he played into your savior complex."

"And I bought it, hook, line and sinker." She plopped the rest of the muffin in her mouth.

"And now you want out?" Shane asked.

Kayla swallowed and took a sip of coffee. "That's not possible."

"Anything's possible. We just have to figure it out."

Kayla rose. "I've said too much. I should go."

Shane quickly stood up and grabbed her shoulders. "If you ask me, you haven't said enough. You've kept it all bottled up and that's not good. You should talk it about. It might make you feel better."

"I should go." Kayla made a move to leave, but Shane had a grip on her.

"You don't always have to be the strong one, Kayla. You can lean on us. We won't let you fall."

Kayla stroked his cheek. "I know that, Shane. If there's one thing I know, it's that I have the best family in the world." She kissed his cheek. "I'll be all right. See you soon."

* * *

"This is not good." Ethan said aloud, looking at the morning's paper. His assistant was kind enough to put the paper on his desk with the entertainment section open. There was a picture of Ethan at the gentleman's club the night before. Kayla was going to be livid. Not only had he not come home last night, but he'd been caught on camera at the club.

It wasn't like he'd done anything wrong. He'd played some pool and had one drink too many and had slept over in one of the private rooms, but that didn't matter, Kayla was going to have him for breakfast. He immediately called her office but was told she was in meetings for most of the morning. He would have to make a preemptive strike and tell her first.

After their argument, this was the last thing he needed. Otherwise, he'd be taking cold showers for a long time to come.

Kayla was happy to get out of the office for lunch. Everyone in the office was gossiping about the paper. Her mother and Piper had left a message for her and she'd been doing her best to avoid Shane and Courtney. Ethan had been caught in a gentleman's club! Kayla knew what happened in places like those and the sort of women that congregated there. No wonder he hadn't come home last night. She'd called her attorney to see if they could use the fact that Ethan had visited a gentleman's club as grounds for a divorce. Alan had agreed that it would certainly raise doubt about whether Ethan was unfaithful. When Kayla hung up, she had some hope that the tide would change in her favor.

She was happy to be having lunch with Ayden that afternoon and have a few hours of normalcy. Right now, her life was a hot mess. Not only did Ethan not love or respect her, he was humiliating her in public. Who knew what other secrets she could unearth and use to her advantage to get out of this marriage and spare her already-bruised heart?

Ayden greeted her with a warm hug and kiss on the cheek. "Kay, thanks for coming," he said as he helped her into a seat.

"It's absolutely my pleasure," Kayla replied. "I'm looking forward to catching up."

The waiter came by to take their drink order and Kayla ordered a ginger ale. Her stomach had been upset after that blueberry muffin and seeing Ethan in the paper.

"Tough morning?" Ayden asked when Kayla remained quiet at the table.

"Something like that." Kayla didn't want to get into her marital troubles, least of all with her ex-boyfriend. "So, tell me what have you been up to all these years?"

Ayden told her about his heading up a new office in London for his company and how his leadership caused sales to jump nearly fifty percent.

"That's wonderful, Ayden."

"And you," Ayden commented, "have been very busy. I've read the papers. You and Ethan Graham? How did that happen?"

"It's a long story," Kayla said.

"Try." He propped his chin on his hands and leaned in to listen.

"The truth?"

"That would be a start."

"Adams Cosmetics was in trouble and Ethan came sniffing around. He pursued me, pretty relentlessly I might add."

"He wanted you," Ayden surmised.

Kayla nodded. "And I gave in."

"I guess I'm not surprised," Ayden said. "You always did have a thing for Ethan."

"I did not," Kayla replied, but Ayden raised his eyebrow skeptically. "Okay, maybe when I was younger, but I got over him. I mean, look how long we were together." She sipped on her ginger ale.

"Yeah, we were together a long time, but I always knew there was something holding you back," Ayden said thoughtfully.

"What do you mean?"

"I always felt like there was piece of your heart you weren't completely giving me, that you were holding back a part of yourself. And now I know why. It was Ethan Graham. I guess I always suspected, which is why I suppose I gave you that ultimatum to come with me to London. And when you didn't…" Ayden shrugged. "Knowing for sure now helps, helps me have closure."

"I'm sorry, Ayden." Kayla reached across the table and touched his hand. "I never meant to hurt you. I guess I didn't know myself."

"And now?"

"Knowing sure hasn't helped me much," Kayla replied. "There's so much unsaid between Ethan and me."

"You can change that," Ayden returned. "Ethan was and is the love of your life, and you have to fight for what you want."

"Love shouldn't be this hard."

Ayden smiled. "C'mon, you know the best things in life are those that we fight the hardest for. So go get 'em, slugger." He lightly punched her jaw.

From across the room, Daniel noticed Kayla having lunch with an attractive gentleman and obviously someone she knew quite well as he greeted her with a hug and a kiss. It could be purely innocent, but given the headlines that morning, was Mrs. Graham making a statement by having lunch with another man? And how was Ethan going to interpret it?

Apparently not too well, because Ethan had a cow when Daniel informed him of Kayla's lunch plans later that afternoon. It was well after three when he'd finally had the chance to make it to Ethan's office.

"Are you sure, Daniel?" Ethan asked.

"Of course. I would never bring this to your attention otherwise."

"So who was it?"

Daniel smiled. He knew Ethan would ask and had tipped the host to tell him who Kayla's lunch partner was. "Ayden Turner."

"Her ex-boyfriend?" Ethan nodded as fury boiled inside him. "You realize she's doing this to get back at me." He paced his office. "She saw this morning's paper and decided she'd get me back by having lunch with her ex."

Daniel jumped to Kayla's defense. "It could be purely innocent, Ethan. There doesn't have to be a nefarious motive here. She could have had this lunch planned weeks ago and the timing is purely coincidental."

Ethan shook his head. "I don't think so. Kayla has been at odds with me for a while. Matter of fact, ever since the night of the launch party, I've noticed her reacting coolly toward me."

"Did something happen that night?" Daniel inquired.

Ethan had racked his mind wondering the same thing and couldn't come up with a single thing he'd done wrong. "No. I made a point of making sure we honored the Adams family tradition by attending Hypnotic's launch together and I stayed by her side the entire night. I don't know what's got

Kayla bent out of shape, but I won't have her disrespecting me."

Daniel laughed. "Well, she could say the same thing about you after seeing this morning's paper. A gentleman's club, Ethan? We haven't been there since you got married. You should know better."

"Don't harass me, Daniel," Ethan replied. He was already exasperated. "Last night I was irritable because Kayla was keeping me at bay and I just went there to have a drink and blow off some steam."

"Then you should show her the same latitude. Perhaps I shouldn't have told you about this lunch, because you're blowing this way out of proportion."

"I am not," Ethan said, "but I am going to have a little chat with my wife." He headed to the door and slammed it behind him.

Daniel sighed. He'd never seen Ethan jealous. If Ethan was jealous that Kayla was out with another man, his feelings for her must run deeper than he had wanted to admit. Kayla was in for a battle.

When Ethan made it to Kayla's office it was nearly five. "Mr. Graham." Myra smiled when she saw him. "Mrs. Graham is in her office."

"Thank you, Myra," Ethan said. "And you are dismissed for the rest of the evening."

"But Kayla wanted me to complete a report before I left."

"That won't be necessary. You can go." He wanted absolute privacy when he spoke with Kayla.

Myra looked up at Ethan and realized he meant business and instantly logged off her computer and started packing up her belongings. She didn't know what was about to go down, but it wasn't going to be good if the thunderous expression on Mr. Graham's face was any indication. "Have a good night," she said, and made a quick exit.

Seconds later, Ethan burst through the door to Kayla's office and she glanced up. "Ethan." She sighed. He was the last person she wanted to see. She wasn't prepared to do battle with him. "What do you want?"

Ethan slammed the door behind him and strode toward her desk. He leaned down until he was eye-to-eye with Kayla. "I want to know why you're having lunch with other men."

"What?"

"You heard me," he said through clenched teeth.

Kayla couldn't believe her ears and pushed back her chair. "So you're having me followed? Are you really that paranoid?" *What other way was there to explain why he knew she'd had lunch with Ayden?*

"Of course not. Daniel was having lunch and saw you."

"And he ran right back to tell you. Great!" Kayla threw down the pen she'd been writing with. "So, you want to get into this right here?"

"By all means," Ethan said, staring down at her icily.

"Fine!" Kayla rose from her chair. "Why don't you explain why you didn't come home last night and were caught in a gentleman's club? How about we start with that?"

"So is that why you went out with Ayden?"

"Don't deflect and try to turn this back on me." Kayla pointed her finger at him. "You started this."

"And you were going to finish it, right?" Ethan returned. He was staring daggers at her. "Why else would you go out with your ex?"

"What does it matter to you?" Kayla replied. "Hell, we have *your* ex spread out on billboards across this city with the Adams Cosmetics logo, and do you hear me whining?"

"You haven't answered my question," Ethan fumed. "Are you still in love with your ex?"

"I don't have to tell you a thing. My personal feelings are my own."

"You're my wife!"

"Ha!" Kayla laughed and faced him like a tiger ready to pounce. "You may have bought me, but I am not your slave, Ethan."

"Kayla, I'm warning you!"

"Warning me?" Kayla seethed with rage and humiliation at his audacity given everything he'd done. "You're not the boss of me. I can have lunch with whomever I please. Matter of fact, I'm done with this conversation. Get out of my office!"

Kayla went to turn her back on him and Ethan swept her in his arms and imprisoned her against his body. "Like hell, you will!" Ethan roared. He bent down and kissed her long and hard.

His kiss both angered and aroused Kayla. "Let me go!" She struggled against him, but Ethan's hold was like a vise. She hated that his mouth was masterful and he used it to give her a hot, yearning kiss that made heat pool in the lower half of her body, especially when she felt him hard against her.

Before Kayla knew what was happening, he was pushing her backside against her desk. He pushed all the papers on her desk aside and they went tumbling to the floor. Then Ethan ripped open the blouse she was wearing with both hands and buttons went flying in every direction. He clumsily worked the silky straps of her bra down her shoulders, exposing her bare breasts to his searing gaze. And then his mouth came down on her, drawing one breast into his mouth. He began sucking on her nipple until it turned into a tight crest.

Kayla didn't know how she moved from anger to lust in five minutes flat. It didn't make any sense what they were doing and where they were doing it. All she knew was that she wanted him naked and inside her. She worked his suit jacket off and tossed it across the room. She tugged his shirt from the waistband of his trousers and pulled it free while he hiked her skirt up to her waist and began fumbling with the scrap of fabric that was her panties.

Ethan lowered them down her legs until he came to the soft tuft of her hair at the center of her thighs. He slid his fingers inside and found her wet and warm and ready. As was he. He could feel his rock-hard erection straining in his briefs. He was happy when Kayla unfastened his trousers and pushed them and his briefs down his legs in one quick movement.

He quickly settled himself between her thighs, gripped her buttocks and thrust inside her, filling her completely and making them one. He secured a handful of her hair in his fist and lowered his mouth again on hers.

Kayla skimmed her fingernails down his back as he gripped her waist and dove inside her. Ethan was exultant that this woman was his and thrust inside her again and again while Kayla chanted his name like a prayer or ritual. Their coupling was fierce as Ethan frantically brought them to fulfillment. When it was over, they gradually slid off the desk and collapsed in a limp heap on the floor, spent.

As she looked up at the ceiling, Kayla was overcome with what had just happened. Not only had she been mindless to where she was and made love in her office, where anyone could have heard or seen them, but they'd just made love without protection.

"That was pretty crazy, huh?" Ethan said finally, but

Kayla didn't speak, so he turned to face her and stroked her cheek. "Are you okay? I didn't hurt you, did I?"

Kayla turned away so he couldn't see tears welling in her eyes. *What had she done? How had she let the situation get so out of control?* She always made a habit out of making sure he had on a condom, but just now, she'd let lust get the best of her and what if… She was afraid to even think of the possibility.

"Kayla." Ethan leaned over and grasped her chin to face him and found her skin wet. "Are you crying?"

"No." Kayla struggled to sit up. She glanced around for something to put on, but her current outfit was in shreds on the floor.

"You're a bad liar." Ethan smiled, sitting up along with her. "Here, take my shirt." He slid it off his shoulders since he was still partially wearing it.

"Thanks." Kayla slid her arms inside the garment and curled her legs underneath her. A million ideas were swimming through her head, many of which had a dancing baby, but she couldn't let Ethan know them. If he thought about it and thought there could be any chance of a baby, he would never let her go.

"When I came in here, I didn't intend for that to happen," Ethan stated, turning to her. "I came in here to throttle you because I was so upset and to explain about last night."

"Don't bother," Kayla said, rising to her feet and heading to the closet near her private shower. She kept a spare suit in her office in case of an emergency and could change into that. No one would ever know that they'd just had sex in her office.

"Kayla, don't you think we should talk about this?"

"Talking is what got us into this," Kayla said. She tossed his shirt back at him as she walked into her private bathroom.

She emerged fifteen minutes later, freshly showered and with her hair brushed back into a ponytail. Ethan had re-dressed and looked as polished as when he had first stepped in.

Being in the shower had given Kayla time to think. She needed to figure out what she was going to do if she were pregnant. She needed an exit strategy and for that she needed to be alone, away from Ethan.

Ethan smiled. "Good thing you have an extra set of clothes." He'd disposed of the outfit he'd destroyed.

"Good thing." Kayla half smiled as she walked toward him.

"So you ready for that talk now?" Ethan inquired. He couldn't read her face. It was expressionless, which wasn't the Kayla he knew. She usually wore her heart on her sleeve and he could read her pretty easily, but this time her emo-tions were masked. It made his mind reel. Had he gone too far?

"Ethan, I need a break from this marriage."

He hadn't expected that statement and it angered him immediately. "If you think I'm going to give you a divorce, you're dead wrong, Kayla. We made a deal." He knew he sounded harsh; he just wasn't prepared to lose her. She meant too much to him.

"I'm not saying I want a divorce," Kayla snapped. She didn't appreciate his tone. "I just need to think, so I'm going to my parents' home for a while."

Ethan thought about what she wasn't saying. "Time to think, you mean you want time away from me?"

"Yes." Kayla forced herself to look at the man she loved, the man whose child she could be carrying. "And I'm hoping you will respect me enough to give me that time."

"Frankly, I don't think it's a good idea for us to be apart

right now. I think we need to figure out what's going on between us, but I respect you enough to give you your space."
Perhaps some time and distance would be good for the both
of them. So when they came back together, they could finally decide what kind of marriage they were going to have
once and for all.

"Thank you," Kayla responded, and walked over to her
desk to grab her purse out of her drawer. "We'll talk soon."

And with those words she was out the door, leaving Ethan
to wonder about the state of their marriage.

Chapter 14

Her parents' home was her second stop. Her first was Piper's apartment. She needed to talk, and despite the abrupt end to their last conversation on the subject, she knew Piper would listen because she was the only one who knew Kayla's true feelings for Ethan.

Piper was surprised when she opened the door and found Kayla on the other side. "Girlfriend, what are you doing here?"

"Can we talk?"

"Of course." Piper ushered her inside. She watched Kayla go immediately to the couch and plop down. "Oh, this calls for some wine." Piper went to walk to the kitchen, but Kayla stopped her.

"I can't have wine, maybe tea?"

Piper stopped short and turned around. She knew what no wine meant. "Okay, I'll be back in a sec."

She returned a couple of minutes later to the living room

and joined Kayla on the sofa. "I turned on the kettle. Now you want to tell me what the heck's going on? Is this about the article in the paper?"

"Not entirely."

"Fill me in."

Kayla sighed. "Where do I begin? Do I start with the fact that I'm in a loveless marriage? Or maybe that my husband is having an affair with our new spokeswoman, his exgirlfriend, or perhaps that I just had unprotected sex with my husband in my office and can now be pregnant?"

"Oh, my goodness!" Piper slouched down on the couch.

"You're telling me," Kayla responded.

Piper ran her hands through her shock of red hair. "Okay, first things first. How do you know he's having an affair?"

"I saw them with my own eyes at the launch party, Piper. She was sidled close to him and poised to give him a big kiss and he didn't push her away. I couldn't bear to watch anymore."

"Did you confront Ethan about his duplicity?"

Kayla shook her head. "I couldn't. If I did, he would know how much he hurt me and I don't want or need his pity."

"Yet you had unprotected sex with him after knowing all this?"

"I know, I know." Kayla dropped her head in her hands in despair. "It's awful, isn't it? That I have no self-control? We got into a fight about the article and my lunch with Ayden and one thing led to another and we were having sex on my desk."

Piper rolled her eyes upward. "Kay, I'm sorry, but this story keeps getting juicier. How did Ayden get back in the picture?"

"Courtney and I ran into him the other day while playing tennis and we just so happened to have lunch today of all days. I wasn't trying to get back at Ethan because of the article."

"But that's how he took it?" Piper asked. "Sounds like he was jealous."

"No, more like possessive. I'm his, and even though he doesn't want me 100 percent, he doesn't want anyone else to have me. So he promptly staked his claim by having his way with me in my office and I foolishly allowed it to happen."

"And now you could be pregnant? Oh, Lord, this is a royal mess."

"What's worst yet is that I love him, Piper. I honestly love him and he doesn't love me," Kayla cried. "And if I'm pregnant with his child, it will be a reminder of what never was and what will never be. I don't know if I can deal with that."

"Oh, Kayla." Piper scooted closer and hugged her best friend. "No matter what happens, no matter the outcome, we will get through this. I promise."

Her father was surprised to see Kayla at the breakfast table the following morning. She'd stayed late at Piper's the previous evening because she hadn't wanted to answer any questions. She'd snuck past Victor to her old bedroom without anyone seeing her, but now it was time to pay the piper, no pun intended.

"Baby girl." Her father kissed her forehead. "I'm surprised to see you home, but happy nonetheless."

"Thank you, Daddy." Kayla gave him a halfhearted smile. She sipped on the tea Victor had made her earlier.

"So how long are you here for?"

"Oh, I don't know, a few days," Kayla replied nonchalantly. She didn't want to get into a long conversation on why she was staying at home.

Her father stared at her. "And Ethan is okay with that?

I know I don't like to be away from your mother for very long."

"Yes, Ethan knows and he's okay with it."

"Well, that's great!" He squeezed her shoulder and reached across the table to pour himself some coffee. "We are happy to have you here, if only for a little while."

"I'm happy to be here, too," Kayla responded. She needed the comfort that being home provided her. She had a lot to think about. Namely, what she was going to do if she were pregnant. *Would she want to keep the baby? Did she want to continue this marriage? And could she, if she were carrying his child knowing that he didn't love her?* She wouldn't be able to stay in a pretend marriage because making love with Ethan in her office could have changed her life forever.

She was mulling those thoughts over when Shane joined them in the breakfast room. "Sis, what did we do to deserve the honor of your presence?" he asked jokingly, though he had some idea why she was back home. He'd seen yesterday's paper and Ethan was in the gossip section.

"Just needed to get away from the old ball and chain." Kayla attempted a joke.

"Are you sure that's all there is?" Shane inquired.

"Yes, I'm sure."

An uncomfortable silence fell over the table. "Well, I have to get going," Kayla said. "Meeting at the office. I'll see you both at dinner." She didn't want to discuss her marriage any more than was necessary especially when she didn't understand it herself.

"Ethan?" Daniel called out when he came to the estate after work because Ethan had phoned in sick two days in a row, which he never did. So Daniel came to see for himself what was going on. When he did, he found Ethan closed off in his study in the dark. He was still in yesterday's clothes, hadn't shaved and an empty decanter of scotch sat next to him.

"Leave me alone!" he roared.

Daniel turned on the light switch, flooding the study with light. "What's going on, Ethan?"

Ethan shielded his eyes with his hand and lowered his head. "I don't want to talk about it."

"Where's Kayla?" Daniel inquired, coming forward to stand in front of him. He couldn't imagine she would allow Ethan to behave this way.

"Gone."

"What do you mean gone?"

"She's decided she's had enough of me and needed a break," Ethan responded and turned his back to Daniel

"So you decided to get drunk alone?"

"That's about right."

"Ethan, listen. I think it's about time you started facing facts."

"Oh, really? And what might that be?"

"That you love your wife," Daniel stated. Ethan turned around and glanced up at him strangely. "Don't look like the idea hasn't crossed your mind. You love Kayla and you're upset that she's gone, so you're drowning your sorrows in liquor."

"Even if that were true—" Ethan pointed at Daniel, or at least in his direction, since his vision was a little fuzzy "—which I'm not saying it is, she doesn't want or love me back. If you could have seen how she looked at me after we made love in her office, it was horrible."

"You had sex in her office?"

Ethan nodded. "Yeah, we both got overcome by—"

Daniel held up his hand. "You don't have to explain to

me. I get the picture. The question is, what are you going to do about it?"

"What do you mean?"

"Are you going to tell Kayla how you truly feel?"

"I can't make someone love me, Daniel. And after what I did to get her in this marriage, how could she?" He sure wouldn't. He'd put her through so much. He didn't deserve Kayla or her love.

"You will never know that unless you tell her."

Daniel had a point, but Ethan wasn't sure he could. He'd never put himself out there for any other woman before. He wasn't even sure of the right words to say. "Thanks, Daniel, I appreciate the advice."

"I just hope you listen to it."

Ethan cleaned up his act and made it to the office the next day. He wasn't much in the mood to work, but he was CEO of Graham International.

He was trying to focus on work, but couldn't stop mulling over what Daniel had said. Was it possible Kayla could love him, too? He was interrupted from his thoughts when Byron Adams stopped by his office. What had prompted Kayla's father to come? As he recalled, Byron had vowed to never come back to GI's office ever again. "Byron, I'm surprised to see you here."

"This is not a social visit, Ethan. I'm here to discuss Kayla," Byron said from the doorway.

"Come in, please have a seat." Ethan motioned for Byron to sit down.

"I'll stand," Byron replied and walked over to the window across from Ethan. He stared out for a long time and said. "I've allowed this farce of a marriage between you and my daughter to go on for too long, but no more." He turned to face Ethan.

"Byron..."

"My daughter is miserable because of you, Ethan, and I can't let this continue a moment longer."

"What goes on between Kayla and me is our business. You have no right to interfere."

Byron shook his head. "I disagree. You made it my business when you forced her into a marriage to save our family's company, and I'm here to tell you that you can have it."

"Have what?"

"Adams Cosmetics," Byron stated. "You wanted it. You can have it lock, stock and barrel. That's what I'm going to tell Kayla, so that she is free to leave you with a clear conscience and find someone who loves her and who she loves back."

"You can't do that!" Ethan rose to his feet. Fear coursed through him. Kayla would listen to Byron because she respected his opinion. She idolized Byron. And if she listened, Ethan could lose her.

"And why the hell can't I?"

"Because I love her!" Ethan roared back.

Byron took a step backward, stunned by Ethan's revelation. "Does my daughter know that?"

"No." Ethan ran his large hands down his face, shaking with fear. "I haven't told her."

"What the hell are you waiting for?" Byron asked. "An invitation?"

"I don't know," Ethan said, grasping his head. Deep down he knew why. He was afraid, plain and simple. He was afraid of being rejected. Whenever he'd offered his love to Carter it had always been met with derision and disdain.

"Well, you'd better figure it out because her ex-boyfriend,

Ayden, is back in the picture and sniffing around again, and I can promise you that if you snooze, you lose." The same thing had happened years ago with him and Andrew Jackson. He and Elizabeth had dated in college, but Andrew had taken her for granted. But Byron realized what a gem Elizabeth was and had swooped in for the kill. They'd fallen in love, gotten married and had three beautiful children, which is why he and Andrew had been enemies ever since.

"I thought you didn't want me with Kayla."

Byron laughed. "I don't, but you were right about one thing, Ethan. This isn't about me. It's about Kayla. You and Kayla. And if you truly love my daughter and she loves you, I won't stand in the way. I want her to be happy."

"Even if that's with me?"

"Yes, even if that's with you."

The rest of the week since she'd been home had continued much as it had in years past for Kayla. She'd gone to the office, stayed late much and then came home to dinner with the family. Everyone seemed to be walking on eggshells around her, maybe because they all knew if there were problems in her marriage; it would not bode well for the company.

It was her father who finally stopped into her bedroom on Saturday morning. He knocked on the door and poked his head inside the doorway. "May I come in?"

"Sure, Daddy." Kayla motioned for him to come in. "What's up?"

"Why don't you tell me, baby girl?" Her father searched her face.

"What do you mean?"

"Kayla." He sat down on her bed. "This is me you're talking to."

"Daddy, please don't go there." She turned away refusing to look at him. If there was one person she had to be truthful with when pressed, it was her father.

"I have to, Kayla." He scooted closer to her on the bed. "I hate to see you so miserable."

"I'm not miserable."

"Yes, you are." He pointed to her. "And don't try to deny it. Why don't we start with why you're back home?"

She swallowed hard and managed the feeble answer, "I don't want to get into it."

"You don't have to tell me, because I already know. You're in love with Ethan."

Kayla turned to face him. Tears bordered her eyes and she smothered back a sob. "How...how did you know?"

Her father brushed away her tears with the back of his hand. "I'm your father and I know you, Kayla. Perhaps better than you know yourself."

"Ethan doesn't love me, Daddy. You and I both know he coerced me into marrying him because he wanted *our* company. He knew I would do anything to keep Adams Cosmetics, even if it meant sacrificing myself."

"And you did that even though I never asked you to. Why?"

"I guess it was easy because I've always loved him," Kayla answered honestly. If she couldn't be honest with her father, who could she be honest with? "I've loved him ever since I was a little girl. And I guess this was a way to have him, even if it was in the wrong capacity."

"Are you sure he doesn't share your feelings?" Byron asked. It wasn't up to him to tell Kayla how Ethan felt about her, but he had to get her to see that there was hope for her marriage.

"Yes, I'm sure. There's a lot you don't know, Daddy." He

had no idea about Noelle and that Ethan had been carrying on with her for Lord knows how long. If he did, he would hate him even more, and Kayla couldn't deal with that, so she remained mum. "I've been giving this some long, hard thought over the last week and I think it's time I asked Ethan for a divorce."

"If you love Ethan, there's still hope. You need to be sure before you end your marriage. You should go and talk to him."

Kayla was surprised to hear her father say she should try to save her marriage. She thought he despised Ethan. "Whose side are you on, Daddy?"

"Yours, of course. I only want what's best for you and what will make you happy. Please take my advice, Kayla. You know I wouldn't steer you wrong."

"All right, Daddy. I'll go talk to Ethan, but I make no promises."

"Kayla, no matter what happens, this family will be okay. I don't want you worrying about what could happen to Adams Cosmetics. You've done enough for this family and this company. We will not have you sacrifice any more for us. He can have Adams Cosmetics. Do what is best for you, baby girl. Promise me you'll take that into consideration."

Kayla crossed her fingers across her heart. "I promise."

When Kayla arrived at the mansion later that afternoon, she found a sports car she didn't recognize sitting outside. It gave her pause. Had she made the right decision to come? Perhaps her father was wrong. Maybe there was nothing salvageable in this marriage and she should just cut her losses. But she'd promised her Dad that she would try and so she would. Slowly, Kayla exited her Porsche and went to meet her fate.

She was in the hall, checking the mail on the console, when she heard someone upstairs. *Ethan was home!* She had to go to him. She had to find out one way or another how he really felt about her. She was walking up the stairs when she encountered Noelle standing at the top of the staircase.

It was jarring to say the least, but Kayla didn't let that deter her. "What the hell are you doing in my house?" she asked once she made it to the top.

Noelle chuckled. "I could ask you the same thing. I'd heard that you'd exited the premises."

"Excuse me?"

"Everyone at the office is talking about how you and Ethan are sleeping in separate homes, and I just came here to see if there was anything that I can do."

"You mean to help yourself to my husband. Do you think I'm a fool? I know what's been going on between you two."

"If you're worried about your marriage, perhaps you should stay a little closer to home," Noelle responded, "rather than blame me for your shortcomings."

"My shortcomings?" Kayla replied. "You're the one who's sniffing around my husband like a cat in heat. Perhaps you should go back to your litter."

"You little witch." Noelle grabbed Kayla by the arm. "How dare you talk to me like that! Do you know who I am?"

"Let go of me." Kayla tried to wrestle her arm free, but Noelle had a good hold of her.

"You don't even have a real marriage with Ethan," Noelle continued her tirade. "He only married you to get your company and everyone knows it. You mean absolutely nothing to him, make that less that nothing."

It hurt to hear Noelle say the very thing she'd thought herself, which was that she meant nothing to Ethan. Her father was wrong and she'd made a mistake in coming.

"You're a despicable human being," Kayla said. "And I don't have to stand here and listen to one more word from you're lying, cheating mouth. If you want Ethan, you can have him." She yanked her arm free, but didn't realize she was so close to the staircase. Before she knew what was happening or could stop it, Kayla felt herself tumbling down the stairs. Seconds later, she was unconscious at the foot of the stairs.

Ethan knew what he had to do. Speaking with Byron yesterday had only confirmed what he already knew. As he pulled into his driveway, he was determined to pull out all the stops to get Kayla back. He was going to wine and dine her and then he was going to tell her that he loved her and couldn't imagine his life without her. He'd already put his plan into motion and called ahead to have a romantic dinner made.

He was unlocking the front door when he heard raised voices inside. As he entered the foyer, he could see Kayla and Noelle at the top of the stairs. What the hell was Noelle doing here, and what was she doing upstairs?

He didn't have time to find out because Kayla came tumbling down the stairs and landed right at his feet. "Ohmigod, Kayla!" Ethan rushed to her side and Noelle came bounding down the stairs.

"Ethan, I…I don't know what happened." Noelle was screeching at the top of her lungs. "We were arguing and I grabbed her arm and…and then she pulled away too quickly…"

"Just shut up." Ethan bent down and listened to Kayla's

breathing sounds and checked for a pulse. When he found both, he reached inside his pocket for his cell phone and dialed 911.

"I...I didn't mean for her to fall." Noelle tried to explain once he was off the phone, but Ethan didn't want to hear it.

"Kayla, can you hear me?" Ethan pleaded in her ear. "Baby, please wake up, I need you." But she was unresponsive. She was just lying there not moving, and it scared the bejesus out of him. He was happy when he heard the sound of the ambulance in the distance. This was all his fault! He should never have brought Noelle into their lives. He just prayed to God that Kayla would be all right.

Chapter 15

"How is she, doctor?" Ethan asked when the E.R. doctor came out to greet him and the entire Adams family, including Piper. Courtney had called Kayla's best friend because she knew Piper would want to be there.

"We're not sure yet," the doctor replied. "She hasn't woken up yet, which isn't good in her condition. Did you know your wife was pregnant?"

"Excuse me?" Ethan was floored. "What did you just say?"

"Your wife is pregnant," the doctor repeated. "I would say about two months along."

"Are you sure?" Piper spoke up. She'd thought Kayla said she'd just had unprotected sex with Ethan a week ago.

Ethan turned and glared at Piper. "Do you know something I don't, Piper?"

Piper shook her head fervently. "No, of course not."

"Is the baby okay?" Ethan asked, turning back to face the doctor. "I mean after the fall."

"For now, yes. The ob-gyn specialist on call tonight will come by and do an ultrasound later. In the meantime, we're running a CT scan to make sure there's no head trauma or concussion."

"That won't harm the baby, will it?" Elizabeth Adams asked. "Because Kayla wouldn't want that."

"No, it won't," the doctor replied.

"Can we see her?" Byron Adams asked. "Can we see our daughter?"

"For a few minutes, but I can only allow one visitor at a time."

Byron walked toward the door first, but then remembered his place and turned to Ethan. "I guess that would be you."

"But Daddy, he doesn't even love her," Courtney spoke up. She was tired of being silent and seeing her sister used. They had more of a right to be there than him.

"Hush your mouth, young lady," her father replied, pointing to Courtney. "You don't know the whole story here."

"Thank you, Byron." Ethan patted his shoulder and rushed inside to check on Kayla.

"Would you care to fill us in, Dad?" Shane returned, turning to his father. "Because from where we stand, Ethan has no place by her bedside. He's the reason she's here."

"He's also the man who loves her."

"Say what?" Piper jumped into the fray. "Are you sure, Mr. Adams? Kayla has always wondered if what she felt for Ethan was reciprocated." Piper felt horrible for revealing Kayla's confidence, but she just couldn't keep silent any longer.

"Oh, I'm sure," Byron Adams stated. "He told me himself."

Shane rubbed his jaw. "I always suspected. Remember, Courtney, I said as much at the wedding."

Courtney nodded as she remembered the conversation they'd shared on Kayla's wedding day.

"But why this whole charade? Why didn't either one of them just admit how they felt? It would have saved them both a lot of anxiety," Shane commented.

"Because sometimes young folks have a hard time getting out of their own way," Elizabeth Adams responded.

"So what do we do now?" Courtney asked.

"Get out of the way and let them find their way to each other," Byron replied. "That is what we can do for your sister."

Ethan walked very quietly into the room because he didn't want to disturb Kayla. She was hooked up to all sorts of machines, but he was only interested in one of them. It was monitoring the heartbeat of the baby. It was strange, because he'd thought about having a child with Kayla before but now it was a reality. They were going to be parents and he would have to tell Kayla. Or did she already know? Is that why she'd left him, because she'd known she was pregnant and thought he didn't love her? No, no, Kayla would never do that. She would never deny him his child, would she?

Ethan grasped Kayla's small hand in his and brought it to his lips. He kissed it lovingly. He had to make things right between them. He had to tell her how much he loved her. Otherwise, he risked their child being brought up in separate homes and he couldn't have that. He wanted his child to be raised in a two-parent home with parents who loved and respected each other and who loved their child. He didn't want any child of his to be raised like he was, by an unfeeling father.

Kayla's eyes began to flutter and she slowly began to open them. "Kayla?" Tears of joy sprung in Ethan's eyes. "Oh, thank God!"

"Ethan." Kayla's voice was barely a whisper. "Where am I?"

"You're in the hospital."

"Wh-what happened?" Kayla looked around frantically.

"You fell down the stairs at the mansion," Ethan replied. "But you're okay."

"Are my parents here?" Kayla looked toward the door.

Ethan nodded. "Yes, your family and Piper are outside. We've all been eager for you to wake up and show us those beautiful brown eyes."

Kayla attempted a halfhearted smile.

"Listen, I have some news for you…" Ethan began.

"News?" Kayla's eyes grew wide with fear.

"It's nothing serious," Ethan assured her, patting her hand. "You have a concussion and they're running some tests…"

Kayla stared back at Ethan, trying to figure out what he wasn't saying. "But there's something else?"

Ethan grinned broadly. "Yes, there is."

"Well? Spit it out," Kayla said. Her stomach was already uneasy from the fall, and he was making it worse. "You're making me nervous."

Ethan grasped both of Kayla's hands in his. "We're going to have a baby."

"Baby?" Kayla's eyes grew wide with fear and she started moving around. She stopped when she noticed the monitor by her bedside. "What baby? What are you talking about?"

"You're pregnant," Ethan said.

"Pregnant." Kayla's mind began to race. How could that be? They'd only had unprotected sex a week ago.

"Yeah, you're about two months along, which means we probably conceived on our honeymoon."

Kayla nodded as understanding dawned. She hadn't thought about that. Of course, it had to be then. She and Ethan had made love dozens of times in Bora Bora, and they'd always been supercareful, or so they'd thought. A condom must have broken. How else to explain that she was pregnant?

"How are you feeling?" Ethan inquired, brushing a tendril of hair off Kayla's face.

"I have a bit of headache and feel a little sore," Kayla murmured, "but otherwise I feel okay, I guess."

"I'm going to get the doctor." Ethan rose from the chair. "Let him know you're awake."

"Ethan, we need to talk about what comes next."

"I know." Ethan kissed her forehead. "And we will. Once you get some rest."

"I'm okay," Kayla reassured her parents a short while later, after the E.R. doctor had given her the once-over.

"Are you sure?" Her mother asked, brushing her hair across her forehead. "We were worried about you."

"I know. And I'll be fine." Kayla struggled to sit up.

"Have you spoken with Ethan?" her father inquired. He hoped the young man had told Kayla how he felt. Life was too short to waste another second.

"You mean did he tell me I'm pregnant?" Kayla asked. "Yes, I know."

"Did you have any idea, darling?" her mother wondered as she fluffed several pillows behind Kayla to help her sit upright.

"I had an inkling, though I didn't think I was that far along."

"Are you happy, excited, indifferent?" her mother asked.

Kayla didn't answer, so her father spoke up. "Elizabeth, give her a chance to process it. She only just found out."

"I'm sorry, darling." Her mother kissed her forehead. "You get some rest and we'll see you tomorrow."

"Okay, I will."

"We love you, Kayla," Shane and Courtney chorused on their way out.

"Get well soon, girly." Piper squeezed her hand. "Because I'm going to spoil this kid rotten!"

Ethan was on his way back into the room to see Kayla when he found Noelle crouching in the corner of the emergency room. She looked a wreck. She had raccoon eyes from her mascara running and her eyes looked puffy. "Is Kayla okay?"

"Yes, she is. No thanks to you. What were you thinking, Noelle?"

"I wasn't," she replied, touching her chest. "I just wanted to talk to you in private."

"Upstairs in my bedroom?" Ethan asked. "What did you think was going to happen?"

"Well, I...I guess I thought things were over between you and Kayla. I'd heard she'd moved home to her parents and I just thought... It was stupid..." Noelle's voice trailed off.

Ethan glared at her. "You thought wrong, Noelle. Kayla and I had a fight, but despite it all, we love each other."

"You love her?"

"Yes, which is why the Hypnotic campaign with Adams Cosmetics will be your last," Ethan responded. "I can't have you coming between Kayla and me. As CEO of Graham International and seeing as Adams Cosmetics is one of our subsidiaries, consider yourself fired."

"But Ethan, the campaign is already underway."

"And we will continue to use you for this fragrance, but not for any future fragrances."

"Ethan, I know I shouldn't have interfered in your marriage and I promise I won't again, but you're making a mistake. I *am* Hypnotic!" Noelle huffed. "You need me!"

Ethan grabbed Noelle by the arm, brought her over to a curtained area and pulled her inside. "You're making a spectacle of yourself, Noelle, and I won't have it."

"I'm irreplaceable. I'm Noelle Warner, Academy Award-winning actress!"

"I know you have a high opinion of yourself, Noelle, but you are replaceable."

"You will regret this!" Noelle said, splicing open the curtain and storming out. "I promise you. I will make you pay."

Ethan returned to Kayla's bedside just as the ob-gyn doctor was wheeling in the sonogram machine. They'd moved Kayla up to a private room and planned on keeping her overnight for observation. "Is everything okay?" He looked at Kayla and then back to the doctor.

"Hi, I'm Dr. Jones," the doctor said, extending her hand, which Ethan shook. "I did a preliminary exam a few moments ago and everything appears fine. We're just checking to make sure the baby is okay and to see how far along Kayla truly is."

"It won't hurt her, will it?" Ethan asked.

"No." Dr. Jones shook her head as she lifted Kayla's gown. "You'll just feel some warm gel," she said to Kayla, "and then just some slight pressure as I move the wand around."

"Okay." Kayla turned and faced the machine. She didn't really feel anything, but when she saw the image on the screen, it took her breath away and she fell back against the pillows as the enormity of what was about to happen hit her. She was going to be a mother.

"I would say you're about eight or nine weeks along," Dr. Jones said, as she moved the wand. She pointed to the screen. "You see that tiny little speck? "That's your baby."

"Ohmigod!" Kayla was completely overwhelmed and she covered her mouth with her hand. "That's my baby." She pointed to the screen.

"It is, and he or she looks just fine."

"Is it a boy or girl?" Kayla asked hopefully.

Dr. Jones smiled. "No, it's way too early to tell, but rest assured you'll be a momma eight months from now. When you get back home and rested, set up an appointment with your ob-gyn. You'll need prenatal vitamins and I might suggest the *What to Expect When You're Expecting* book. It's great for new moms."

"Thank you, Dr. Jones, for the advice," Ethan responded.

Once the doctor had gone, Ethan knew it was time he and Kayla had that long overdue heart-to-heart. "Can we talk now?"

"I'm pretty much a captive audience hooked up to these machines, so there's no time like the present," Kayla said. "Why don't I start first?"

"No, let me," Ethan said, sliding over on the doctor's stool until he was by her side.

"Why do you always have to run things?" Kayla asked, exasperated. "Why can't you follow sometimes?"

"Because what I have to say can't wait," Ethan returned unapologetically. "I love you, Kayla Adams!"

"You love me?" Kayla couldn't help but start laughing. "You have to be kidding me."

Ethan paused. Kayla's reaction wasn't exactly the one he'd expected when he said those words for the first time in his life. And he had to admit, he was hurt. "Do you think I'm joking, Kayla? Because I'm not—I love you. I know I railroaded you into marrying me and I didn't give you any time to think, but I just had to have you."

"You mean you had to have Adams Cosmetics," Kayla replied. "And what was I? Icing on the cake?"

"No." Ethan shook his head. "It was nothing like that. Look, I admit I went about this marriage all wrong. And yes, I did want AC, but not at your expense. I've always wanted you. I think I knew it when you were seventeen, but you were too young, so I backed away, filling my life with other women and empty relationships because none of them were you. It's why I've never been able to truly commit to another woman. You stole a piece of my heart when you fell off that horse when you were nine and never returned it. My heart is yours, Kayla."

"And you expect me to believe you now just because I'm pregnant? After everything we've been through? After Noelle?"

"I'm sorry about Noelle and that your fight with her is the reason you and our child are in this bed, but I can promise you she won't be a problem for us ever again. I've fired her."

"Is that right?" Her voice dripped with sarcasm.

"I don't like your tone, Kayla. Why are you so angry with me?"

"Oh, so I finally get to speak?"

"Jump right in." Ethan stood up and paced the floor. "You obviously have something you want to get off your chest." He knew he shouldn't be upsetting her after a concussion, but he couldn't understand her negative reaction to his declaration of love.

"I sure do," Kayla said, pushing the pillows back so she could sit up. When Ethan made a move to help her, Kayla stopped him. "Don't. I can do it myself." She would have to learn, since she would have to take care of her and her child by herself.

"Okay, so speak."

"You were relentless in your pursuit of me," Kayla replied. "You were determined to make me admit that I was not immune to you physically. You kept hounding me until I gave in and I did. I couldn't resist you. Why? Because I love you. I always have. And now we have a child together. And since I'm carrying our child, I have to look out for it, which is why this marriage is over."

Ethan was perplexed. "How can you say you love me in one breath and say you want to divorce me in the other?"

"Because I saw you with Noelle, Ethan!" Kayla yelled back.

"Saw us? When? Where?" Ethan's mind raced to remember a moment that he was alone with Noelle that Kayla could have misinterpreted.

"At the launch party," Kayla replied bitterly. "I saw her in your arms, and that's when I knew I'd been living a childhood fantasy, wanting my Prince Charming to love me back. I realized then that the fantasy wasn't real and that I had to let it go."

Understanding dawned on Ethan. That's when he'd felt Kayla begin to distance herself from him. He'd known something wasn't right but hadn't been able to pinpoint it. "You have it all wrong, baby. Nothing was going on between me and Noelle."

"I know what I saw."

"Did you see me kiss her?"

Kayla searched her memory and he was right. She hadn't

seen them kiss, but that didn't mean anything. "Well, no," she huffed. If she had seen it, she would have bum rushed them. "But you were cheek to cheek. It could have happened after."

"Noelle and I are not carrying on some lurid affair behind your back."

"Then why was she in our house?" Kayla yelled.

"I don't know," Ethan responded honestly. "But I can assure you that Noelle and I are not an item. Matter of fact, check with Daniel, I've been a wreck without you. Hell, check with your father—he'll tell you I told him I loved you."

"I don't know." Kayla shook her head. Her head was swimming. Her father had encouraged her to save her marriage. Could she believe Ethan? Could she trust that what he was telling her was real and true?

"Kayla." Ethan bent to his knees and grasped her hand in his. "I meant what I said. I love you. I'm sorry that I hijacked you into this marriage, but I love you and I don't want to live my life without you, without him or her." Ethan ran his hands across Kayla's now-slender stomach. "Please tell me that you believe me. That you believe we can have a life together."

"Ethan, we got started on the wrong foot in this relationship and have had so many misunderstandings, I don't know if we have what it takes to make a marriage work."

"We can if we try," Ethan said. "No one said marriage was going to be easy, but we have the building blocks, Kayla." He touched her cheek. "We have love."

Kayla looked away.

"Don't do that." Ethan turned her head back to look at him. He needed to look deep in her brown eyes because he needed her to believe him. "Don't turn away from me, from us, from love. You love me and I sure as hell love you. We belong together."

"Maybe we do now," Kayla said, "but with Adams Cosmetics always hanging over my head, we will never be equal."

"Then it's yours," Ethan announced, standing up. "I'll sign all the shares back over to you and your family right now."

"You would do that?" Kayla asked, stunned by the lengths he would go to convince her of his love and devotion.

"Of course," Ethan said. "I would do anything for you." He reached for his phone and started dialing Daniel. If that's what it took to convince Kayla, the mother of his child, that he loved her beyond a shadow of doubt, then that's what he would do.

Kayla's heart rejoiced, because it was in that moment that she knew Ethan loved and respected her. The fact that he would give her Adams Cosmetics without a second thought showed her just how much he loved her and the lengths he would go to to keep her. She reached across and grabbed the cell phone out of his hands. "I don't need the entire company back—I just want half a share, so that we have an equal share with equal say in how we run the company, because this is a partnership."

"That's right. We're partners in love," Ethan said as he bent down and kissed her.

* * * * *

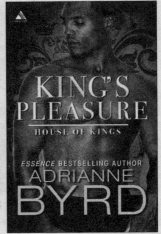

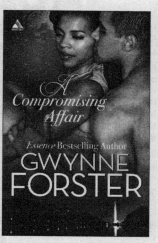

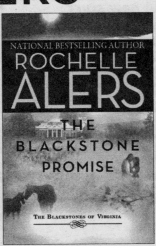

REQUEST YOUR FREE BOOKS!

2 FREE NOVELS
PLUS 2 *FREE GIFTS!*

KIMANI™
ROMANCE

Love's ultimate destination!

YES! Please send me 2 FREE Kimani™ Romance novels and my 2 FREE gifts (gifts are worth about $10). After receiving them, if I don't wish to receive any more books, I can return the shipping statement marked "cancel." If I don't cancel, I will receive 4 brand-new novels every month and be billed just $4.94 per book in the U.S. or $5.49 per book in Canada. That's a saving of at least 21% off the cover price. It's quite a bargain! Shipping and handling is just 50¢ per book in the U.S. and 75¢ per book in Canada.* I understand that accepting the 2 free books and gifts places me under no obligation to buy anything. I can always return a shipment and cancel at any time. Even if I never buy another book, the two free books and gifts are mine to keep forever.

168/368 XDN FEJR

Name	(PLEASE PRINT)

Address	Apt. #

City	State/Prov.	Zip/Postal Code

Signature (if under 18, a parent or guardian must sign)

Mail to the **Reader Service:**
IN U.S.A.: P.O. Box 1867, Buffalo, NY 14240-1867
IN CANADA: P.O. Box 609, Fort Erie, Ontario L2A 5X3

Not valid for current subscribers to Kimani Romance books.

Want to try two free books from another line?
Call 1-800-873-8635 or visit www.ReaderService.com.

* Terms and prices subject to change without notice. Prices do not include applicable taxes. Sales tax applicable in N.Y. Canadian residents will be charged applicable taxes. Offer not valid in Quebec. This offer is limited to one order per household. All orders subject to credit approval. Credit or debit balances in a customer's account(s) may be offset by any other outstanding balance owed by or to the customer. Please allow 4 to 6 weeks for delivery. Offer available while quantities last.

Your Privacy—The Reader Service is committed to protecting your privacy. Our Privacy Policy is available online at www.ReaderService.com or upon request from the Reader Service.

We make a portion of our mailing list available to reputable third parties that offer products we believe may interest you. If you prefer that we not exchange your name with third parties, or if you wish to clarify or modify your communication preferences, please visit us at www.ReaderService.com/consumerschoice or write to us at Reader Service Preference Service, P.O. Box 9062, Buffalo, NY 14269. Include your complete name and address.

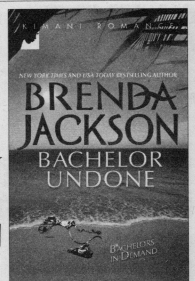